SCARY BOOK OF
Christmas Lore

SCARY BOOK OF
Christmas Lore

50 Terrifying Yuletide Tales from Around the World

Tim Rayborn
Illustrations by Neil Evans

CIDER MILL PRESS

BOOK
PUBLISHERS

Table of Contents

Introduction

Ah, Christmas and all the other December holidays! A time of joy, happiness, feasts, mirth, convivial gatherings, and good feeling all around. In the Northern Hemisphere, it's a time to celebrate the darkest nights of the year with light, food, music, and hope for the season, as well as to ring in the new year.

But it's also a time of cannibals, kidnappers, horrific monsters, ghosts, torture, zombies, demons, blood and gore, and all sorts of other nasty and terrifying things. As we delve into traditional December celebrations, especially in Europe, we find that there is no shortage of tales meant to terrify right alongside those meant to warm the heart (or perhaps, roast the heart until it is well done!).

In this book, we'll peel back the layers of Christmas cheer and see what's hiding underneath, infesting the darkest corners of the cellar and lying in wait in the frozen forests for the unsuspecting, the misbehaving, and the disbelieving. A whole horde of horrors lies just outside the mortal realm, ready to spoil your holidays in the most appalling ways possible!

We'll meet Krampus, the most popular holiday demon of them all, and look at his nefarious deeds—all in the service to St. Nicholas, of course. But did you know that he has many counterparts, spread all across Germany, France, Austria, the Alps, and beyond? There are an astonishing number of variations on the theme of a dark companion to St. Nicholas, and this book will highlight just a few.

We'll also venture into the winter darkness of Iceland, where the ogress Grýla waits to snatch up naughty children in a bag and take them back to her volcanic lair to boil them up in a tasty holiday stew. And if she isn't bad enough, just wait until you meet the Yule Cat!

Or maybe you'd like to answer the door and see a horse skull on a stick, its eye sockets decorated with Christmas ornaments. Be ready to trade clever verses with the revelers, or you'll owe them food and drink. That's Mari Lwyd, coming to a Welsh town near you!

If you live in the Balkans, you might have good reason to fear the Kallikantzari, horrifying creatures who will cause no end of troubles in your home if you don't take precautions and basically bribe them to leave you alone.

Why are there all of these scary stories and creatures? Shouldn't the holidays be a happy time? Yes indeed, but recall that in earlier times, the long part of the year was dreaded by most who lived in northern, colder climates. Survival through the long, dark months was not guaranteed, when food supplies could run out and sources of heat could be scarce. So, it makes perfect sense that fear of creatures that personified the dangers of the winter and the darkness would take hold in the popular imagination.

The celebrations of Yule, Christmas, the solstice, and the New Year were all meant as a respite from the terrors of the time, but these were ever on the edge of the mind, and the village, waiting to claim the unwary on a bitter winter's night. Scary holiday lore still fits right alongside conviviality in the minds of many. These folktales and beliefs were passed down for generations and often enacted in pageants and festivals as reminders of winter dangers, or at least as preludes to the fun that followed.

Some of these legends and celebrations probably had their origins in pre-Christian beliefs, which were later either tolerated or altered to fit into a more Christian framework. Many festivals all but died out, only to be resurrected over the last few decades as symbols of regional tradition and pride. For many in the Germanic regions of Europe especially, it simply wouldn't be Christmas without monsters and mayhem.

It's in the spirit of that relationship that this book presents these wonderfully weird and terrifying tales and creatures. So have yourself a scary little Christmas and read on to learn about the many nightmares lurking in the holiday dark.

St. Nicholas and the Butchered Children

Turkey

Since St. Nicholas is at the heart of many of these tales and legends, we'll begin our journey down the dark paths of Christmas terrors with him.

St. Nicholas, or St. Nick, is a handy alternate name for Santa Claus, but there really was a St. Nicholas, who lived in Asia Minor, in what is now Turkey, from about 270 CE until his death on December 6, 343 (December 6 is still his feast day). In his own time, he was Nicholas of Bari, a Greek bishop in an age when the Roman Empire was not officially Christian, or even close to having a majority of Christians in its population. Not too much is known about his actual biography, but quite a few legends sprung up about him during and after his life. Many of these stories tell about his generosity and his secretly giving gifts to people or money to those in need. He was quite possibly the first Secret Santa!

One such story says that he prevented three girls from being forced into prostitution by dropping sacks of gold through their window each night for three nights, which allowed their father enough money to pay dowries for them. The father discovered him on the third night, but Nicholas told him not to tell anyone about this generosity. Nicholas was also said to have performed miracles, such as calming a stormy sea while he was sailing to the Holy Land, and driving out demons. But the most famous legend about him concerns the fate of three children and a very evil butcher.

The story goes that these three kids were out in the fields and lost track of time. They came to a town and to a butcher's shop, which was lighted inside. They were tired and hungry, and now they were lost, so they knocked on the door. The butcher answered, and they asked him if they could have some food and a place to sleep for the night. He was only too happy to welcome them in, but he had no intention of giving them a warm welcome. Taking out a sharp knife, he killed and butchered each of them, dismembering them and placing the body parts in a barrel with brine for curing. He intended to sell the pieces as ham to unwary customers when the curing was finished (it brings to mind the story of Sweeney Todd!).

A long time went by (some accounts say as much as seven years), but Nicholas learned of the crime and went to the butcher. He commanded that this evil man open up his salting barrel, and the butcher could do nothing but comply. Once open, Nicholas made the sign of the cross over it and commanded the children to rise. The three dismembered bodies were miraculously repaired and the children brought back to life. No word on what happened to the butcher, but later legends say that he was forced to work with Nicholas ever after as penance for his sins. We'll meet some of his incarnations in this book.

This weird legend seems to be a fairly late addition to the stories about Nicholas, probably originating in the Middle Ages, but from it, some began to see Nicholas as a patron saint of children. This, combined with his reputation for gift-giving, dovetailed nicely with winter traditions of presents and miracles, such that Nicholas now has pride of place as a holiday gift-giver in many European countries on December 6, even if he is accompanied by that miserable old Krampus! Which is who we're meeting next, incidentally...

Krampus

Bavaria, Austria, Slovenia, Croatia, and Northern Italy

Krampus is, of course, the granddaddy of all European winter holiday monsters: a fearsome, furry demon with a terrible attitude that can't wait to get out in the snow and cause mischief. He's certainly not the oldest beastie haunting the holidays, but these days, he's definitely the most famous, so it's natural to begin our ghoulish gallery with him.

Krampus accompanies St. Nicholas and has his very own night—the eve of St. Nicholas Day, in fact: (the night of December 5.) Krampusnacht is the time when he is most active, and when children have the most to fear. He is often depicted as a horned, satyr-like, goat-footed demon, carrying a large basket on his back, into which he will toss naughty children to drag them off to terrible tortures. He usually drags chains and carries a *Rute*, a bundle of birch branches that he uses to swat misbehaving children. If that's all they get from him, they should count themselves lucky!

His name might come from the old Bavarian *krampn*, meaning "dead," or the German *kramp*, meaning "claw." Either word seems like a good etymology for him. He has long been associated with St. Nicholas, and tales of Krampus and his punishments might date back as early as the seventh century, though it seems that the earliest written records of this frightening figure date to the end of the sixteenth or the early seventeenth century.

It's possible that fears of a menacing Alpine winter visitor predate Christianity, and that the legends and festivals were

intertwined with Christian belief when the church realized that they couldn't be eliminated entirely. So this fearsome night creature was given a holy role within the church to punish sinners, especially children. The Nazis banned Krampus celebrations, but the people were having none of it, and as soon as those losers were dispatched, Krampus came right back, bigger than ever.

Today, of course, there are Krampus celebrations all across the Alps and beyond (even in the United States). They start in early December and extend into January, no longer limited to one night, which is a great thing! There is no shortage of people willing to dress up as Krampuses (Krampi?) and take part in parades and other big holiday get-togethers, posing for pictures, scaring kids, swatting tourists with fake birch switches, and having all sorts of fun. Dozens of people might show up dressed in their Krampus costumes, ready for a ghoulish party! Krampus is an institution now and a big business, though in the villages and more remote areas of the Alps celebrations tend to be smaller and more traditional, with just one costumed demon accompanying the beloved saint as they make the rounds from house to house, checking in on the behavior of the local children.

Variations on Krampus are many, and we'll look at some of them in the following pages. They are united by the idea of a menacing monster that threatens naughty children with torture and worse, and that often accompanies St. Nicholas, or sometimes other holy men. The blend of the blessings and the curses is a common theme, with the idea being that those who have been good will get what they deserve, as will those who haven't...

In recent years, Krampus has become something of a holiday classic, starring in horror movies, music videos, and more. This obscure figure from the frozen mountains of Europe has taken the world by storm!

Frau Perchta

Austria and Bavaria

Frau Perchta, or simply, Perchta, is a bit of a mystery. Some suggest that she was once a goddess in pagan Germanic times, one that the people viewed favorably. She might be a version or variation of any number of other Germanic goddesses whose legends spread throughout Germany and beyond in the times before Christianity. Or she might have been seen as a guardian spirit of some kind. She is first mentioned, disapprovingly, around the year 1200, and might have been a figure that was still venerated or placated in some ways. But, as often happened, the church was not thrilled with the idea of reverence of a rival spirit, much less a god, and probably set about blackening her name until such time as she was taken down a peg or two and made into a fearsome winter witch, accompanied by demons and other creatures of the darkness. Oh, and she also has a charming nickname: "the Belly Slitter."

A few centuries later, we find the words *Perchten* and *Perchtenlaufen* referring to ceremonies or processions in the Tyrol area of Austria that featured some of the demons and ghosts what we've come to associate with these holiday-time monster mashes at these holidays. In legends, they were demons and ghosts that roamed the night skies. And a demon named Percht seems to have become a Krampus-like figure. Did Perchta give her name to these celebrations? Quite possibly. The twists and tangles of the history of these mysterious beings are confusing and will probably never be unravelled. But at some point, Frau Perchta became another of those creatures that haunts the night.

She came to resemble the classic stereotype of an old crone or witch: dressed in rags, holding a cane, old and wrinkly, but also

sometimes having a beaked nose made out of iron. And she would often carry a knife or other dangerous weapon with her. She loved spinning (which might give her an association with the old Germanic/Norse goddess Frigg) and keeping things tidy. According to legend, wool or flax had to be spun and ready to weave by January 6. And for those who didn't have it ready, there would be some nasty surprises in store. She might visit the house and set fire to any fiber not yet spun. Worse, the householders had better have tidied up and left out a bowl of porridge for her.

But if someone scoffs at this or forgets the oatmeal, old Frau Perchta will fly into a rage, burst into the bedroom, disembowel the offender, and fill their empty abdominal cavity with straw and rocks. Happy New Year!

When she's not busy ripping guts out of lazy housekeepers, she is sometimes said to ride with the Wild Hunt, accompanied by the Perchten (more on them later), on page 33. The sounds of wind and thunder are their noise, not anything as mundane as the natural elements. While Krampus focuses his evil on the early part of December, Frau Perchta prefers the Thursdays before Christmas and the whole of early January, which is one way to tell them apart. Well, that and the whole disemboweling thing. But maybe Krampus is into that, too—who knows?

Frau Gaude

Germany

Frau Gaude is especially well known in south-central Germany. In some ways, she is similar to Frau Perchta; there are many regional variations on the theme of a night witch that brings trouble and death. She is known to haunt the towns and villages of the area during the Twelve Days of Christmas, along with a pack of ghostly hounds. Legends say that she is doomed to wander with them forever, because once, as a mortal, she made the foolish wish that she could hunt forever. She got that wish; for much of the year, she rides with the Wild Hunt, and some tales even say that she leads it.

During the Christmas holidays, Frau Gaude wanders about at night looking for homes with open doors and windows. If she finds one, she will send one of her dogs inside, where it will make itself at home. As long as the residents do not disturb it, nothing much will come of this. But if they do bother it or try to drive it out, disaster will strike. The dog might grow angry and attack the homeowner, even tearing them apart. And if the homeowner tries to kill it, the best that they will accomplish is to see it transform into a rock that will stay in that form until midnight each night. Then it will become a dog again, and likely a very angry one. It will howl at those who tried to kill it, and each of these howls is a curse that will affect the unfortunate villager. The curses can be anything from poor health to accidents, bad luck, or even death. Once Frau Gaude "blesses" you with one of her hounds, you're stuck with it!

And if the dog curses you, only Frau Gaude can remove the curse, but she will only do so once a year, on Christmas Eve, so if you are suffering from any kind of affliction, you'd better be ready on that night and hope that she hears you and agrees to help you. Some say that she only helps because she was once worshipped in ancient times, and desires to take people's attention away from their Christian faith by only offering her aid on that night. But whatever her motives, it's best to make sure that your doors and windows are securely shut each night during the Christmas season, so that you won't be hit with a dog's curse and have to beg for relief the following year!

Frau Gaude might have been a goddess; some say that she was the wife of the god Odin/Woden. One of her other names is Frau Wode, or Mrs. Woden. Some go even farther and speculate that she is merely Woden in disguise.

Another related frau is Herke, who, like Gaude, is usually seen in the company of hounds, and, like Perchta, is concerned that everyone finishes their spinning on time—or else there will be consequences. As you can see, these legends overlap and often are simply variations on each other, with similar themes and always the warning to watch yourself and behave during the holiday season.

The Night Folk

Germany, Austria, and Switzerland

At the intersection of Germany, Austria, and Switzerland, unfortunate people could sometimes catch a glimpse in wintertime of a mysterious and macabre procession: the Night Folk, also sometimes known as the Night Throng, or, even more charmingly, the Death Folk or Death Throng. Unlike the Wild Hunt (see page 53), this group does not fly about chaotically in the sky or engage in overt violence. They are a solemn procession of lost souls and perhaps other beings from beyond the veil. They most often wear all black, such as robes and shrouds, if they are seen at all. Sometimes one merely hears them, most often with music.

Indeed, the Night Folk often appear with haunting music playing, melodies that can be sweet and strange enough to entice mortals to follow after them. In this, the Night Folk are similar to the fairies of Ireland and Britain, who would sometimes lure mortals into their circles or their realm with enchanting music. Such mortals were usually never seen again. The Night Folk might even offer to teach new songs and new instrument skills to the unwary, but it's always best to say no.

It was said that in the alpine areas—at the holidays especially—one needed to be on the lookout for the Night Folk. It was foolish to try to block their ghostly march, and if they processed toward a house or some other building, one always needed to open the doors on both sides to let them pass through. If not, disaster and ruin might befall the house or its owners. If the Night Folk were left alone, they would often leave those around them alone in turn. But not always.

In some regions the Night Folk could be relatively harmless, a sad procession of beings doomed forever to wander the land, denied eternal peace. But in some areas, especially in Switzerland, they could be outright malevolent if crossed. Here, the Night Folk often processed without music (or, at least, it was less enticing) and could herald plagues and disasters.

One legend told of a man who encountered the procession after hearing the sound of a bowed instrument. He happened to catch sight of Death playing a violin and leading a long crowd of the Death Folk. The man saw many of his neighbors in the procession, who were still alive. At the end, he saw himself! And so the prophecy came true, as one by one, each of those neighbors died of a plague, and he was the last to die of it. Well, that would ruin the holiday celebrations, wouldn't it?

It was best never to gaze upon them if one could help it, for one would already know they were coming by their sound, which could be anything from pleasant to horrible, from singing to drumming to strange drones to the sound of rattling bones. Their presence often predicted the year to come; beautiful music meant that it would be a good year, while a cacophony meant that it would not. But really, most people lived in the hope that they would never hear the Night Folk at all!

Türst

Switzerland

There are many fearsome spirits that travel in the wilds of the winter darkness. In Switzerland, there's a hunter who rides in the nights before and after Christmas and who goes by the name Türst. As a kind of one-being Wild Hunt (see page 53), he's especially known and feared in the area around Lucerne and the nearby Mount Pilatus, but he also appears in other places from time to time.

Türst carries a hunting horn, which he blows to announce his arrival. He has a pack of hunting hounds, each of whom only has three legs, and these creatures are led by a dog with only one eye in the middle of its forehead—a terrifying sight, indeed! In some legends, this leader is a strange and bizarre mixture of a dog and a pig. There are some tales that say Türst himself can transform into a dog for his hunt and that he will lead his dogs across the sky in this form.

Like the Night Folk, one must stay out of his way if he and his pack are on the move, for to impede his progress would be to invite terrible luck. Those who are foolish enough to bar his path—intentionally or otherwise—or try to keep him from hunting will risk being transformed into one of his dogs and joining his ghostly hunt forever. It's said that even cows and livestock will scramble out of the way if they see Türst coming, and if they are in any way touched by the hunting dogs, they will either go crazy or stop giving milk forever. So, farmers and herders must make sure to leave their barns open if Türst's pack is on the way.

Türst's hunting horn can summon any number of other strange creatures to join him on the hunt, and he is also said

to be the master of the goblins who live in the Santenberg Mountain near Lucerne. Strangely enough, these creatures and Türst are believed to guard a unicorn that lives in the mountain, which seems like a strange task for an evil group of spirits, but so be it!

Türst and his fearsome pack are likely a localized version of the Wild Hunt (see page 53), one can also think of him as a personification of the fierce winter storms and the gales that can blow through the Alps. His hunt is accompanied by strong, howling winds and sometimes snow. The people are right to fear him. To try to stave off some of his ferocity, villagers would put up *Wetterkreuze*, or "weather crosses," which were said to repel him, or at least lessen his effect, and perhaps calm his deadly winds.

Türst is yet another of the winter spirits who was feared during Christmastime and reminded people that they were always at the mercy of the elements. Leave him alone, and he'll likely do the same. Interfere with him in any way, and it could cost you your life.

Sträggele

Austria and Germany

Sträggele is a German version of the Italian word strega, or "witch," and she is said to sometimes accompany Türst on his nightly hunts. If Türst is bad, Sträggele is much worse! She is said to be hideous and repulsive to look at, and not someone you would want to meet, much less cross. She goes out on Ember-night, the Wednesday before Christmas and, like Frau Perchta (see page 16), she is obsessed with finding out if children and young women have finished all of their spinning. And if they haven't, well, they are in for a potentially dreadful fate. Sträggele has a taste for human flesh, you see, and will be only too happy to snatch up misbehaving children and gobble them up. So kids had better have done all of their chores and finished their spinning work...or else!

It's not quite clear why she would accompany Türst on a hunt, when her main concern was order in the home, but some traditions say that they are married. We could be looking at a surviving legend about Woden, the one-eyed god. Many of these winter figures might have originate from legends of this ancient and revered figure, known as Odin in Scandinavia. Indeed, Türst's one-eyed dog could well be a remnant of an older belief that changed quite a bit over the centuries, but never fully disappeared, even if it was only remembered in folktales and legends.

Sträggele's (and other fraus') obsession with spinning could be a reference to the work of the old goddess Frigg, Woden's wife, and goddess of hearth and home. Though in early pagan belief there was nothing hideous or evil about her, over time, and with creeping Christianization, she might well have been transformed into a terrible old hag, and found a new life in the form of the various Christmas witches and female spirits that haunt the living with the threat of a gruesome death.

At the very least, she was one of many supernatural beings whose presence could make children behave, not just at Christmas, but throughout the whole year. And yet, in some cases, Sträggele might be kind and generous, especially if the children had done all of their work and spun all of their spinning. So, we see the familiar pattern that shows up so often in these creepy holiday folktales: treats and presents for the good and punishment for the bad, which also plays out in modern celebrations, even if only in fun.

Belsnickel

Germany, France, Switzerland, and Pennsylvania Dutch Country

Belsnickel has a bit of an attitude, to be sure. Stories about this Christmas curmudgeon originated in southwest Germany, especially in the area along the Rhine River. Like many of these mysterious holiday horrors, he is a companion to St. Nicholas, but in Belsnickel's case, he travels alone. His name refers to the fur he wears (*Bels*) and his connection to Nicholas (*Nickel*). He also wears rags and sometimes women's clothing, and occasionally deer antlers on his head. Sometimes he is called the "Christmas Woman," which makes for an interesting exercise in cross-dressing, a tradition that has long associations with the chaotic celebrations of the season in various countries.

Some traditions also say that he wears a mask with a rather grotesque long tongue, which clearly connects him to Krampus.

Belsnickel travels on his own, but with much the same intention as other companions of St. Nicholas. He shows up a week or two before Christmas, and comes to reward the good children and punish the bad, but he does it in his own special way. In his pockets he has candy, nuts, and cakes, but he also carries a switch to administer beatings. Who will get what? That remains to be seen!

When Belsnickel arrives, usually after dark, he will rap on the door or a window with his switch. When a child answers, Belsnickel will either ask them a question or demand that they sing a song for him. If he likes what he hears, he will toss treats to them. But if they try to catch these goodies too quickly or too greedily, they might still get a swat with his birch! He might ask children what good deeds they've done in the past year. Again, if they can't remember, or their deeds aren't especially impressive, they might get another swat! He's a rather grumpy fellow who doesn't need much of an excuse to administer punishments. He served as a reminder to children that they still had a little time to be good before the big day, i.e., Christmas. Getting swatted was a warning to amend their ways.

The Belsnickel tale is one of those legends that was for many years enacted as part of the holiday celebrations in Germany. Men dressed up as Belsnickel would travel from house to house in their villages and offer treats to the children, and perhaps give them a playful swat with a soft birch. Indeed, it was so popular that it was brought to America by German immigrants in the nineteenth century. In these communities, Belsnickel was much more important than Santa Claus, even if he had a similar function.

In Pennsylvania, he was known as Pelsnichol; in Maryland, he was called Beltznickle. The tradition of him visiting houses during the holidays continued until the end of the nineteenth century, when it began to die out in favor of more typical American-style celebrations. Happily, in recent years there have been attempts among folklorists and enthusiasts of old traditions to revive this one, so it might yet make a welcome return. German cultural societies in Pennsylvania and elsewhere are including Belsnickel in their holiday celebrations, proof that the crotchety Christmas Woman will live again for a new generation.

Knecht Ruprecht

Germany and the Alps

Knecht Ruprecht is one of the more benign companions to St. Nicholas, relatively speaking. He often resembles Nicholas a little, being dressed in a dark robe with a pointy hood that sometimes has fur trim. He has a big bushy beard and carries a large sack, which might make him look something like a folkloric or rustic Santa Claus, but, of course, he also often carries a switch like so many of the other sinister companions to St. Nicholas. And we know what that will be used for! Other versions of the character have him holding a staff, and perhaps having bells attached to his robe, so that he jingles as he approaches. But is that a jingle of celebration or dread?

Unlike Krampus, Knecht Ruprecht almost always appears alone with St. Nicholas, so in present-day parades and celebrations, you won't find dozens of people dressed up as him all traveling together. There is only one Knecht Ruprecht; Krampus, on the other hand, often travels in herds! Sometimes, Knecht Ruprecht's face has ashes smeared on it, a reminder of older traditions such as mumming (see page 96), or attempting to hide one's face from evil spirits. But in recent decades, this makeup has caused some controversy because of the potential for such depictions to resemble blackface (see Zwarte Piet on page 70 for more on this).

According to tradition, Knecht Ruprecht would sometimes carry a bag of ashes, and ask children to pray. If they couldn't or wouldn't do so, he would swat them with the bag instead of a switch. This might explain why he sometimes had ash all over his face!

Knecht Ruprecht also carries a switch. But instead of disciplining naughty children the way Krampus does by swatting them with the switch or dragging them off, he will often simply hand the switch to the child's parents to administer the punishment themselves. Nice of him, eh?

Some scholars have suggested that Knecht Ruprecht has a darker origin and that his original function may have been something more like Krampus. Indeed, he might actually be a variation, in his own unique way, of Krampus, though he is only first mentioned in processions and celebrations from the seventeenth century. It's possible that he is a demonized version of an old, forgotten pagan figure. He might represent something like a satyr, a dwarf, or some sort of pagan being who once wandered the land in the days before Christianity. Some scholars have likened him to a German house spirit, like a kobold, elf, or goblin.

But these days Knecht Ruprecht is a gift-giving, faithful servant of St. Nicholas who doesn't actually deliver any punishments on his own. The two of them often show up together in modern celebrations, going door-to-door in German and Alpine villages and offering gifts to children. And yet, he might still carry the switch as a reminder of his past.

Knecht Ruprecht is definitely not Krampus and he's probably one of the more friendly versions of the creepy characters that you'll encounter in these dark holiday celebrations, but he might well have developed from a figure who was a lot more sinister a long time ago.

Schönperchten and Schiachperchten

Austria

The Perchten (plural of Perchta) are said to accompany Frau Perchta (see page 16) on her nightly jaunts, and perhaps her belly slitting activities. They are her assistants; maybe they hold down victims while she disembowels them? It seems like it might be a team effort. More recently, this collection of helpers has appeared in two types: Schönperchten ("Beautiful Perchten") and Schiachperchten ("Ugly Perchten").

Whatever their origins, it seems that each group had its own functions during the holidays. While Frau Perchta was out and about, checking up on spinning and chores and brandishing her sharp knife to those in need of it, the two groups of followers went about different activities, especially on the nights following Christmas.

The Beautiful Perchten engaged in benign behaviors, wandering through towns and villages and bestowing gifts on random people. These could be material things like money or other wealth, or it might be something intangible, such as good luck.

Those who were fortunate enough to encounter one of the Schönperchten might count themselves especially lucky not to have met the Shiachperchten instead. The Ugly Perchten also sometimes worked for the benefit of the people, but not in such nice ways. The Schiachperchten were much more Krampus-like in their appearance and mannerisms, often having hooves and carrying sharp whips. Their purpose was to howl and scream and drive away evil spirits.

It's worth noting that these two types of Perchten seem to have only come about in the mid-nineteenth century, or perhaps a little earlier. Prior to that, there were only Perchten who accompanied the Frau on her grim quest to seek out victims. One theory for this late arrival is that there had long been a practice of village men dressing up like Perchten, wearing masks with fangs and ugly visages. They would go around from house to house to cause trouble and general mayhem. They would howl and scream, and in so doing, hoped to frighten away any evil spirits that might be present in someone's home. While it was all meant in good fun, things almost certainly got out of hand, especially if any of these revelers had had too much to drink.

The introduction of Schönperchten and Schiachperchten into the festivities might have been a way to control that a bit more. It doesn't seem that these particular types of Perchten existed in folklore. If so, they have not been recorded. So traditions developed that allowed for the Perchten to bring blessings and to drive away nasty spirits in slightly less frenzied way. Indeed, in certain areas of Austria and elsewhere, there are now processions, held on January 5, of costumed Perchten that bring holiday cheer and drive away evil, without the potential raucousness and law-breaking that afflicted some celebrations in times past. Those dressed up as Beautiful Perchten wear elaborate and stunning headgear, often illuminated and colorful so that they show up in the night from a long distance away. Such parades represent an interesting attempt to "tame" the wilder side of some of these Christmas legends and the horror that surrounds them.

Rauhnacht

Germany

Depending on which tradition and location you are study-ing, Rauhnacht is either the time between Christmas and Epiphany (i.e., the Twelve Days of Christmas), or it starts a little bit earlier, on December 21, and goes through the same period. The tradition of observing Rauhnacht is strongest in Bavaria. It's thought that the word might mean "smoke night," and refer to an ancient practice of burning some kind of pro-tective herbs or incense to protect against the evil spirits that walk the earth at this time. Alternately, it might mean some-thing like "rough night," and refer to the rough and unsavory creatures that roam the world, or at least those folks who dressed up as them for pageants and festivals.

Celebrations of Rauhnacht can be dated to the early eighteenth century, and they continued up until World War II, when the Nazis banned them (like everything else enjoyable). It's only been in the last forty years or so that these festivities have been revived, often with great spectacle. Some celebra-tions, such as at Waldkirchen, include the firing of cannons to frighten away evil spirits (no simply shouting loudly for this lot!) and the appearance of many Krampus-like costumed characters to entertain, scare, and delight onlookers. These festivities are not exactly revivals of ancient traditions, but more often modern presentations of a collection of folklore brought together in ways that they might never have been done in previous centuries.

Children and others might go door to door seeking sweets, again, rather like trick-or-treating. Traditionally, they were likely to be given a kind of jam donut called a *Rauhnudl*, though these days, candy is a perfectly acceptable substitute—probably because a pile of donuts would get messy and sticky very quickly!

Tradition says that laundry should never be left out on a line during Rauhnacht, because if the Wild Hunt (page 53) happens to ride through, some of the spirits might get caught on the clothesline and be unable to free themselves. Despite the potentially hilarious imagery that this calls to mind, this would be bad, for said spirits would be doubly angry and might hang around the offending home and cause no end of trouble throughout the coming year. Even worse, one of the "Fraus" that rides with the Wild Hunt might take up a piece of clothing and make a shroud of it, which would be intended for one of those who lives in the offending home. In other words, leaving out your sheets to dry could lead to one of the spirits leaving you out to dry.

Villagers traditionally burned smoke and incense to keep spirits away, and a tradition of developing skills with a whip developed, again with the thought that the sound would frighten away any evil that might venture too close to the house.

People also honed their divination skills, especially fortune telling with melted lead, which was called Molybdomancy. On New Year's Eve, people would sit around a table and, using a candle flame, melt lead in a spoon, which they would then pour into a bowl of water. As the lead cooled in the water, it would form shapes, which could be interpreted by those in the know. Lead prediction is still popular, and you can even buy kits to do it with, though they're usually made with wax or perhaps tin these days, given that lead isn't the safest material around. Or maybe that's just what the evil spirits want you to think.

The Knocking Nights

Austria, Germany, and Switzerland

The Knocking Nights, or Klöpfelnächte, take place on the three Thursdays before Christmas. They were celebrated in southern Germany, Switzerland, and Austria, though "celebrated" might not be the right word. They were first mentioned in the mid-sixteenth century in a poem by German writer named Thomas Naogeorgus, where he describes how on the three Thursday nights prior to Christmas, village boys and girls would run about knocking on doors and windows, wishing well to their neighbors and sending blessings. But of course, it wasn't always about fun and good cheer.

These nights, rather like the twelve nights after Christmas, were a time when the spirits and ghosts walked the earth and supernatural things could happen, whether you wanted them to or not. The name itself probably originally came from the practice of knocking on the walls of barns and other places for livestock. This would cause the animals to start making noise, whether "moos" or "baas" or "neighs," what have you. Animals were also said to have been given the gift of speech at this time of year, by the way. By knocking and listening to the sounds the animals made, people might actually learn something of the future. They might even be told about it in their own language.

One consequence of this is that said farmers might actually learn who is going to die in the coming year, which could be a good thing or a bad thing. One can recognize how this could've gotten out of hand as a superstitious prank, when people would listen to animals and then start claiming that other people in the same group would not live out the year. You can easily imagine a bunch of kids doing this and trying to scare

each other silly! No doubt it didn't go over well with a lot of families and religious authorities.

The Knocking Nights could, as Naogeorgus wrote, involve kids dressing up as ghosts and going around to knock on buildings to make noise and cause trouble. Again, we see something similar to Halloween. The young offenders would then run away and hide so that when the person opened the door or window, they wouldn't see anyone. Yes, this was a stupid prank, but it was meant to bring good luck to the house; if your home were to receive a knock from one of these jokers, it would actually be a good thing.

Some children even carried long poles to rap on doors and windows, after which they would hide. Sometimes their poles had spikes on the end, and by knocking, they would be rewarded by the owner of the house, who would put a small bit of cake or even a donut (there are those donuts again!), or possibly some cheese or meat on the end of the sharp stick. The kids would go away with something tasty to eat. But, of course, sometimes things took a turn for the worse and angry villagers might take offense, or accuse innocent children of something they didn't do. Or maybe they accidentally damaged a door or window and ended up in trouble with the law.

As such, there were many attempts to bring the knockers under control. By the seventeenth century, the church was trying to ban the practice of knocking and replace it with pageants that recreated Mary and Joseph's journey to Bethlehem. More pious, perhaps, but it took a lot of the fun out of the whole thing! Recent revivals of the Knocking Nights have also included the almost obligatory Krampus and other Christmas beasties.

Pelzmärtel

Austria and Germany

Pelzmärtel appears on the eve of St. Martin's Day, which is November 11, so he gets the scary Christmas season off to a good, early start. He's both a gift giver like St. Nicholas, and someone who scares people, like Krampus and other creatures of the night. He wears furs and old, ragged clothes. Sometimes he is seen sporting a long beard and a soot-covered face, and bells adorn his costume and jingle as he walks, warning of his approach. His name seems to be a combination of *pelz*, "fur," and Martel, or Martin's name.

On the Eve of St. Martin's, he was said to wander the villages of western Bavaria, where, unlike some of his other frightful counterparts, he would scatter candy out for children to pick up. Now, this might sound very nice, but it wasn't actually meant to be a selfless gift. Instead, he used the candy as bait, and when the children ran out to retrieve it, he would swat them with his switch, whether they were naughty or nice!

In modern St. Martin's celebrations, Pelzmärtel's swats are light and playful, and are not meant to hurt anyone. Of course, in some cases during celebrations of the past, things could get a little carried away, and the practice itself might well derive from old folktales about being wary of taking candy from strangers. This tradition of good-natured swatting seems to have been pretty popular in Bavaria throughout the nineteenth and early twentieth centuries, particularly in the town of Wassertrüdingen. Like so many of these German traditions, Pelzmärtel celebrations disappeared during World War II, but have been revived since the 1970s.

These days, the tradition is alive and well in certain regions, and the Martel characters are played by enthusiastic revelers in long coats, with all of the classic Pelzmärtel trimmings. They often toss out nuts to children, which are sometimes known as Nußmärtel, or "nut Martels." As always, Pelzmärtel swats all children, whether they've been good or bad. It might be more based on how quickly kids go and retrieve the treats that he throws for them. But if a child is swatted by the switch, it's considered good luck, so he or she has nothing to lose by rushing out to retrieve Pelzmärtel's nuts and/or sweets.

This luck-giving gift might also be related to an old tradition about the so-called "Martin switches," which cowherds and other herdsman gave to their employers. St. Martin's Day was a traditional day for bringing cattle in from the fields for the winter. So herdsmen would give their employers these switches out of gratitude for their wages. They were also said to represent good fortune for all involved, and would be hung in the home for luck throughout the season. They were then used in the spring to bring the cows out to the fields once again. It seems that, whether herding cows or children, these particular switch-related traditions are surprisingly well-intentioned.

Wild Barbaras

Bavaria

On the night of St. Barbara's Day (December 4) in a few places in the Bavarian Alps, an unusual group of women will appear. They are known as *Bärbele,* or the Wild Barbaras. They will be dressed in old-fashioned peasant clothing and usually also wear aprons and headscarves. They carry brooms and switches and wear a cowbell or two at their waists. They have on grotesque-looking masks that are mixes of all sorts of components, such as acorns, pinecones, moss, and leaves, all put together to make them look like old crones or witches. But those wearing these masks are usually young women in their teens, or possibly a little older (but certainly at least sixteen). They represent St. Barbara, who was martyred as a teenager, and they come to remind villagers of her suffering.

Depending on the town you're in, dozens of these Barbaras can come through at one time. They will reward children with treats such as apples or cookies and maybe nuts, and also give these treats to the children's mothers. Interestingly, instead of punishing bad children, the Wild Barbaras normally only swat young men, which is a refreshing change! But again, these blows are not meant to punish, but to the bestow good luck. The masked girls may even hit their intended victims until they do something, such as a dance, in response. Once the Barbaras are satisfied that their "swatee" has done enough, they will move on.

In some villages, the Wild Barbaras will go into various homes and use their brooms to sweep the house in order to remove evil spirits and shoo them outside. The Barbaras can only do so much, however, and there are certain kinds of evil spirits that will not be dislodged, no matter how much sweeping they do. These pesky entities require the presence of St. Nicholas, who will come two days later to bring even more blessings (after Krampus has taken away all the bad children, of course!).

This folk practice seems to be very old. But, like so many of these pageants, it disappeared in the twentieth century, only to be revived in the last few decades. It seems that the legend of the Wild Barbaras might date back to the Middle Ages. The legend's origin doesn't seem to be pre-Christian, but rather it's a holiday celebration that made use of older ideas and folded them into a newer Christian theme.

There is a medieval fortune-telling practice connected with St. Barbara's Day and it's somewhat like the lead divination of Rauhnacht (see page 35). But in this case, people look at flowers from a fruit tree that they bring inside. It might be an apple or a cherry tree, or some other suitable species. The idea is that the indoor heat will make these trees bloom, and the number of buds and flowers that appear will be an indication of the kind of year coming up. Hopefully, they will bring good luck. People have used these buds to try to determine if they will have a good harvest or a successful business. Young women traditionally used them to find out if they would get married. The use of flowers is based on a legend about how, when Barbara was martyred, a small branch she had kept with her in her prison cell bloomed at the moment of her execution (by beheading, in case you're wondering).

Bloody Thomas

Bavaria

And the monsters just keep coming! On the night of December 21 (around the winter solstice), a terrifying creature was said to emerge from the forests of Bavaria. Known as Bloody Thomas, or sometimes Thomas with the Hammer, he was a fearsome, ogre-like fiend that carried a blood-drenched hammer. Bloody Thomas shares his name with St. Thomas, the disciple whose feast day is on December 21, so the connection between them seems obvious enough. But unlike "doubting Thomas," the disciple who needed to touch Jesus's wounds to believe, Bloody Thomas doesn't seem nearly so well-disposed toward the everyday people of the region.

Like many other creatures of winter, Thomas will punish those who have done wrong. We can assume that his bloody hammer demonstrates the way in which he'll do it! It's thought that the idea for this monster might have come in part from the tradition of slaughtering animals for winter on December 21, which is also a day to begin making the sausages that are so beloved in the region. Does Thomas wield his hammer to smash unwary and misbehaving children and tenderize their meat for his own hellish sausages? Brats made into brats? We can only speculate.

The legend of this fearsome creature inspired the local tradition of a cruel prank on St. Thomas' Day: pretending to be Bloody Thomas to scare children. A farmer or other laborer might pour animal blood from the slaughter over his feet or legs and head off home to scare his own children, or perhaps those of his neighbors. He would bang loudly on the door, threatening to smash skulls or other body parts if the children

misbehaved. He would then force the door open a crack and thrust one gore-covered foot or perhaps one bloody leg into the cottage, just enough to terrify the little ones into being good and obeying their parents, if they wanted to live to see another day. He might even wear a hideous mask and peek around the door, giving the children a glimpse of his face and probably eliciting screams. Yes, it's horrible, but also a bit funny! Presumably, the children were scared enough to be good for the rest of the holidays, perhaps enough so that they earned some presents and other treats.

Legends about Bloody Thomas and the customs associated with him mostly died out over time, as these things often do, though in a few scattered places in Bavaria he might show up from time to time as a companion to St. Nicholas and Krampus in pageants and parades, strangely, as a monstrous bird. But in earlier times, he was yet another frightening reminder of what might lurk in the darkness of the forest, and a warning not to stray too far from home, lest he return on December 21 and claim you for his grotesque pantry!

Schmutzli

Switzerland

Schmutzli is something of a recent phenomenon in the collection of twisted holiday characters on display here. A helper for Samichlaus (the Swiss Father Christmas), he only really came into existence in the early part of the twentieth century, when he was known as Butzli, but this name was changed at some point. Of course, he might have existed in some form at an earlier time. "Schmutzli" refers to the dirt (Schmutz) and ash that are smeared on his face, another reminder of the older traditions of people darkening their faces in rituals and pageants to ward off evil spirits.

Schmutzli is very similar to Père Fouettard (see page 64), though Schmutzli is common in German-speaking parts of Switzerland, while Père Fouettard haunts the French-speaking regions. Schmutzli carries a broom along with a switch and usually a sack as he accompanies Samichlaus on his rounds through the towns and villages. And, of course, he threatens misbehaving children with the switch or the sack, just as Krampus and so many other holiday demons do. Children should recite a poem for him and tell him the good deeds they've done in the past year, otherwise he might snatch them up into his sack and take them out to the forest. There, they will sit until they've learned their lesson, rather like an elaborate (and chilly) version of sitting in the corner! And if these children don't change their ways, they might be left out there forever!

In some areas, Schmutzli also seems to be an incarnation of the wicked innkeeper who butchered the boys that St. Nicholas later saved (see page 64), and for his penance he must forever roam the snowy paths of Switzerland with the saint. Another legend says that he was originally a woodcutter who recovered Samichalus's gifts after he lost some of them when a hole tore in his bag. For this deed, Schmutzli was rewarded by being made Samichalus's companion.

Schmutzli and Samichalus traditionally traveled around with a donkey; not as elegant as flying reindeer, perhaps, but more suited to the Alpine regions. But unlike Krampus and some other evil holiday entities, Schmutzli seems to have taken on a more benign role in recent decades, essentially acting as Samichalus's assistant in bringing toys and sweets to all children. But his somewhat foreboding appearance remains and links him to many of the other Germanic creatures of the night who haunted children's dreams, whether naughty or nice. There have been reports of some Schmutzli celebrations getting out of hand, and those playing the character (especially if they are teenaged boys and young men) taking it all too seriously and trying to thrash bystanders with their switches. Modern sensibilities and law enforcement take a dim view of this, of course.

Regardless of his current version, Schmutzli is a reminder of those evil forces that held everyone in their grip in the cold months of the year, and even though there have been attempts to rehabilitate some of these creatures to make them friendlier to modern sensibilities (and let's be honest, to tourists), there are some who prefer their Christmas entities to be horrifying rather than cute.

A Host of Holiday Horrors

Beyond Krampus, Perchten, witches, and cannibals, there were any number of other creatures that stalked the darkest nights of the Germanic winter landscape, waiting to lure the unwary to their doom. Here are just a few of them:

The Drude was an evil spirit or hag that tried to cause sickness or even smother people in their sleep. She could be driven off by a *Drudenfuß*, or "Drude's foot," a pentagram that frightened away nocturnal horrors. Her name might derive from Thrud, the daughter of the Germanic/Scandinavian god Thor, demonized over time into a night terror. In some areas of

Bavaria, it was traditional to hang up a *Drudenstein*, a stone with a naturally formed hole in the middle. This little rock was said to help ward off nightmares and, presumably, suffocating hag demons.

The Habergeiß is usually described as a three-legged goat (one leg too few) or bird (one leg too many), with glowing eyes. Or it might be a goat with bird feathers (why not both?). It often appears with Krampus, but also sometimes on its own. Traditionally, seeing this creature or even hearing its cry was a bad omen, and if that weren't bad enough, it would sometimes resort to vampirism, drinking blood from both farmers and their animals. In festivals, it would carry a *Zistl*, a kind of basket, on its back. As with so many of the other holiday monsters, this basket was used to carry off badly behaved children.

The Seelvogel, or "Seabird," is a flying phantom whose task is to transport the souls of the dead to the other side, like an avian Grim Reaper. It resembles the Perchten in some legends, and is still portrayed today in various Alpine and Germanic festivals, where it is usually represented by a macabre bird's head on the end of a pole, rather than a whole costume. Needless to say, in older times, you didn't want to hear this bird's call, because it meant that your time was up.

The Howagoas might confront the unwary at any time of year, but seems to have been especially feared in the darkest nights of the year, and its appearance might be marked by a bone-chilling wind. It looks like a goat, though it's said to have a cackling, otherworldly laugh, and might also croak like a toad. As if all this wasn't bad enough, it wanders through towns and forests, sometimes waiting in haystacks or at crossroads to prey on foolish mortals who cross its path. It is said to accompany Krampus on his sinister journey from time to time, but also engages in evil acts of its own, such as spoiling grain, causing nightmares, scaring children, and even predicting death.

These are only a small number of the hidden horrors that might come out to confront the living during the holiday season, but they were joined by many more, some of whom have been lost to time. No matter. There are enough remaining tales of eldritch beasties to keep modern readers entertained and chilled well into a dark winter's night.

The Original Nutcracker

Germany

The Nutcracker is probably the most famous ballet in the world, and a holiday tradition that millions around the world love and look forward to seeing each year. Even those who don't enjoy ballet appreciate this one, or at least pretend they do. So you might be surprised that, when it premiered in 1892, it was a bit of a critical flop, which was disappointing to its composer, Pyotr Ilyich Tchaikovsky. He was hired to write it, and agreed to do so if he could also show his opera *Iolanta* as a double feature. That's right, a ballet and an opera in one concert! The Russian tsar attended the premier and enjoyed the ballet, but critics were less kind, calling it childish and even tedious. They also insulted the dancer playing the Sugar Plum Fairy, which seems very Scrooge-y! As if that wasn't bad enough, the dancer who played the Nutcracker later killed himself with a razor, to avoid arrest.

The story itself is much older than the ballet. It was written in 1816, and was called *The Nutcracker and the Mouse King*, which sounds familiar enough, but there were many differences.

The author, Ernst Theodor Wilhelm Hoffmann (1776–1822), liked to write about inanimate objects coming to life, which explains the *Nutcracker* theme quite well. In his story, the girl is not named Clara, but Marie. She lives in a restrictive household and likes to escape into her dreams. But these are not always happy dreams, and sometimes they are filled with strange and grotesque imagery. They are more like nightmares, but she still prefers them to her waking life. In this story, she dreams of a nutcracker coming to life, and once he does, he goes to battle against a hideous seven-headed rat king. Marie is injured, falling and cutting her arm badly on some broken glass from a cabinet.

When she tells her family about her dreams, they forbid her to speak of them, so unsettling are they. But Marie protests that she would rather marry the nutcracker and live in that bizarre world than the one that she's trapped in. She eventually gets her wish. The nutcracker comes to life, and she decides to leave with him and go off to the land of her dreams, with all of its wonders and terrors.

Alexander Dumas, author of *The Three Musketeers*, decided to rewrite the story in 1844 to make it more family friendly, and it was this version that Tchaikovsky used when composing his ballet. In recent years, some dance troupes have brought back some of the imagery from the original story, including the seven-headed rat king, but will anyone ever be bold enough to bring all of Marie's holiday nightmares to life on stage?

The Wild Hunt

Germany, England, Scandinavia, and Beyond

The Wild Hunt is a classic motif of folklore that has been adapted by many different cultures and nations over the centuries, most notably in northern Europe, and is usually revisited in the winter months. There are many variations, but the core of the myth is a vast, spectral army that rides through the night at certain times of the year. Those unfortunate enough to witness it risk getting caught up in it and dragged away, to become a part of the hunt and ride forever with its ghostly companions.

Different traditions of the hunt have different leaders. In Scandinavia and Germany, its leader is often Odin, or Woden, the one-eyed god of Germanic and Nordic myth. Jacob Grimm (of fairy tale fame) hypothesized that tales about the Wild Hint might have existed in pre-Christian times. He believed that they originally referred to processions of the gods, who would come to our world at certain times of the year to bestow gifts and blessings. With the rise of Christianity, this procession took on a demonic character, and the hunt became something to be feared, populated as it was with evil spirits, nightmarish steeds, goats from hell, and all manner of evil things. Grimm's view was and is not accepted by everyone, but traditions of a nocturnal procession of other-worldly beings do seem to be quite old.

From England, there is a fascinating entry in the *Anglo-Saxon Chronicle* about an event at Peterborough in 1127 that occurred around the time of a disputed appointment of an abbot. Several people saw ominous riders one night: "Think no man unwor-

thily that we do not say the truth; for it was fully known over all the land that, as soon as he came thither, immediately after, several persons saw and heard many huntsmen hunting. The hunters were swarthy, and huge, and ugly, and their hounds were all dark and broad-eyed, and ugly. And they rode on black horses, and black bucks. This was seen in the deer-fold in the town of Peterborough, and in all the woods from that same town to Stamford. And the monks heard the horn blow that they blew in the night. Credible men, who watched them in the night, said that they thought there might well be about twenty or thirty horn-blowers."

Whatever might have happened here, the Wild Hunt became known as a bad omen. While Odin was its leader in Scandinavia, in Germany, Perchta (who we've met—see page 16) could also be one of its leaders, while in France, the figure was sometimes known as Hellequin, or the Erlking. In Wales, Gwynn ap Nudd, the Lord of the Dead, leads the hunt with his nightmarish hounds. In England, the god Woden often led the hunt, but legends also spoke of Herne the Hunter and even King Arthur himself directing the hunt; who knows what leader those credible folks in Peterborough saw? All over Europe, different bands of hunters haunted the night sky, often in winter, sending more than a few chills down the backs of the locals and prompting many of them to stay safely inside during the long, cold nights of the season. Do your holiday shopping during the day, or else you might end up the victim of a terrible fate and wander the world forever in the company of some truly frightening beings!

Victorian Christmas Ghost Stories

England

Of course, we all know Dickens' *A Christmas Carol*, the classic tale of the miser Scrooge and his redemption after three ghosts visit him, remind him of his past, show him the suffering all around him, and then reveal to him what will happen if he doesn't change his ways. It's one of the most famous and best-loved books in the English-speaking world and beyond, a classic that is read and enjoyed every year.

But what many people don't know is that the Christmas ghost story was a staple of late Victorian holiday tales, and people loved to read and listen to scary stories of ghosts and hauntings set during the chilliest days of the year. The cold weather, the gloomy fog, the bare trees, the snow-covered ground...all of these made for fertile imagery for tales of spooks and delight. And as we've seen, the season seems to bring out the most terrifying tales in many lands!

Dickens himself edited magazines such as *Household Words* and *All the Year Round*, and the Christmas editions of these publications almost always included ghost stories contributed by various authors. He stopped work on these in the late 1860s, and left behind the idea of ghostly stories. He once wrote that he feared "I had murdered a Christmas number years ago (perhaps I did!) and its ghost perpetually haunted me." But by then, the idea had taken hold with readers, who were eager for more.

Authors such as Walter Scott, Elizabeth Gaskell, and Arthur Conan Doyle all contributed to the demand, with a flair for the dramatic, purple prose galore, and more than a few frights. Consider excerpts like this one from Ada Buisson's "The Ghost's Summons": "Suddenly I aroused with a start and as ghostly a thrill of horror as ever I remember to have felt in my life. Something—what, I knew not—seemed near, something nameless, but unutterably awful." This passage calls to mind the later works of H. P. Lovecraft and his descriptions of unspeakable cosmic horror, and yet it is firmly set at Christmastime.

Or how about this one, from "Horror: A True Tale" by John Berwick Harwood: "In the sickly light I saw it lying on the bed, with its grim head on the pillow. A man? Or a corpse arisen from its unhallowed grave, and awaiting the demon that animated it?"

The humor writer Jerome K. Jerome wrote about the popularity of ghoulish seasonal tales in his book from 1891, *Told After Supper*: "Nothing satisfies us on Christmas Eve but to hear each other tell authentic anecdotes about spectres. It is a genial, festive season, and we love to muse upon graves, and dead bodies, and murders, and blood."

Well, alright then.

These stories are not what we might expect to go along with our eggnog and Christmas cookies, but they were most definitely a popular part of the Victorian holiday celebrations. We might think such tales have more place at Halloween, and that's because that is the exact shift that occured. By the early twentieth century, interest in Christmas ghosts was waning (except for Dickens' novel), while in America, Halloween was becoming the time when all things spooky would be celebrated, thanks in part to Irish and Scottish immigrants, who'd had a long tradition of recognizing late October spirits and thin veils between the worlds. But that's another tale for another time.

Mari Lwyd

Wales

The procession of the Mari Lwyd is one of the more fascinating and creepy customs to be associated with the Christmas holidays—a Welsh tradition that has seen renewed popularity in recent years. Mari Lwyd is usually a mare's skull draped in a white cloth and set on a pole, carried by one person hiding under the cloth. The carrier can control the movements of the skull, and even make it snap its bony jaws at unwitting people passing by. Mari Lwyd is usually decorated with ribbons and color for the holidays, but that doesn't take away from her ghoulish appearance; lights or Christmas ornament balls are usually set into the eye sockets, just for added horrid effect!

As you might expect, the name Mari Lwyd has an uncertain origin. It might mean "gray mare." There are several light colored horses in Celtic mythology (both in Britain and Ireland) that have various abilities and can sometimes cross back and forth between the lands of the living and the dead. Another possible translation (and tradition) is Gray Mary, which posits a Christian origin for the creature. It tells the rather sad story of a pregnant mare that was let out of the manger to make room for Mary and Joseph. She had to find a new place to give birth.

The practice of carrying the Mari Lwyd was first recorded in 1800, in a book titled *A Tour through Part of North Wales* (by one J. Evans), though it might well have existed for a lot longer. But the creature might not have pagan origins, in any case. Many scholars now believe that Mari probably only dates to the sixteenth century, as it has features in common with

other "hobby horse" traditions that became popular across England then.

This tradition is basically a mumming, wassailing, or caroling celebration taking place during the Twelve Days of Christmas, where the holders of Mari Lwd take the skull from house to house in the village, starting at sunset. Mari Lwyd isn't always the only unusual figure in the group. There might be other recognizable figures, such as jesters, Punch and Judy, or other stock characters. They will go to a house, knock, and ask to be let in, singing traditional Welsh songs. But it's the home-owner's responsibility not to let them in, responding in song. And so the contest and the fun begins. The Mari Lwyd and the homeowner might offer up *pwnco*, rude poems and rhymes to try to outdo each other.

If the owner of the home finally gives in and accepts defeat, they are expected to let in the revelers and offer them some food and ale for their efforts. Once inside, Mari might snap at children, either scaring or delighting them. In fact, it's in the owner's best interest to do so, since having the Mari in one's home guarantees good fortune in the coming year. Then the revelers will leave and go to the next house, and start all over again. One would imagine that they might be pretty full and inebriated by the end of a Mari Lwyd run!

Needless to say, this creepy caroling session wasn't always popular with ministers in the nineteenth century, some of whom wrote damning condemnations of it. But though it waned in the twentieth century, it has seen a renewed popularity in tthis century, ensuring that the mare skull and her obnoxious handlers will continue to brighten (darken?) towns in Wales and beyond for many years to come.

The Nuckelavee

Orkney Islands

The Nuckelavee is a terrifying creature that haunts the winter landscape of the Orkney Islands, off the coast of northern Scotland. Though it lives in the sea, it is known to roam the land as well, and the cold months of the year are its time to be free. During summer, it is held at bay by the Mither o' the Sea (Mother of the Sea), the primal force that keeps the forces of the tempestuous ocean in check. But she has no power in winter, so then the powers of evil and chaos are once again unleashed. The only saving grace is that the Nuckelavee despises rain and fresh water, and cannot come ashore when it's raining.

This horrifying creature is the stuff of nightmares, and was definitely believed in and feared by the Orcadians until at least the nineteenth century. The threat of its very presence could dampen anyone's holiday spirit. Tradition and those who claimed to have seen it described it as manlike, but with a single red eye, an enormous mouth, and no skin. Its muscles and blood were visible and its sinewy arms hung down to the ground. Sometimes, it was said to ride a horselike monster that looked similar—i.e., skinless and terrifying. Even worse, some accounts combined the two creatures into a monstrous hybrid, like a centaur from one's worst nightmare. Even worse than that, one description said that the manlike torso grew out of the back of the horse and that they were fused.

Though the monster was perhaps at its most powerful in winter, it could emerge at any time after summer's passing. If crops failed, animals fell ill, or accidents happened, locals would often blame the Nuckelavee. Orcadians had a practice

of drying kelp from the sea and not only using it as a fertil-izer, but also burning it and using the ash for glass-and soap-making. But the smell of burning kelp was said to enrage the Nuckelavee, which hated it with a passion. In retaliation, it would sometimes send a deadly disease that would kill horses. Nevertheless, kelp burning continued in defiance of the beast's rage until the nineteenth century.

The nineteenth-century Orkney folklorist Walter Traill Denni-son recorded an interview with a man, Tammas, who claimed to have seen the Nuckelavee one dark and moonless night, but who was quite reluctant to talk about it. Still, he described his experience of being out late and glimpsing a monstrous shape in the distance. As it drew closer, he realized it was none other than the fearsome creature, and it looked just as described here: a horse-human hybrid, skinless, with one eye and a ter-rifying air. He knew he couldn't outrun it and would probably die, but he was able to flee from it only because he caught some fresh water from a nearby loch on his foot and it splashed on the creature, enraging it. Then he bounded over a running river, which it wouldn't cross. It let out an awful howl, furious because it was only able to grab the man's cap.

Did Tammas really see the Nuckelavee, or was he perhaps a bit under the influence? And if he was telling a tall tale, why do it, when he didn't even want to talk about it to begin with and had to be persuaded? Tammas probably did see something and believed it to be the Nuckelavee. Maybe it was just an angry man on horseback. Or, maybe not...

Père Fouettard

Eastern France, Belgium, and Switzerland

Père Fouettard is yet another of those "helpers" of St. Nicholas who is anything but helpful! His name means "Father Whipper" or "Old Man Whipper," which fits his job description. Like others in Nicholas's entourage, Père Fouettard accompanies the good saint on December 6, with the intent of dispensing lumps of coal and/or beatings to naughty children. He is known and feared in eastern France, as well as Belgium, and parts of French-speaking Switzerland.

According to folk tradition, Père Fouettard was once an innkeeper who was a murderer and possibly a cannibal. He was said to have captured three boys on their way to a religious school and robbed them and killed them. In some versions, he and his wife cut up the bodies and put them in a barrel. This intersects with the miracle of the St. Nicholas legend, when he discovers the crime and brings the children back to life. In this medieval French version, Père Fouettard repents his evils and Nicholas commands him to join him on his journeys to atone for his sins.

Another origin story places Père Fouettard in 1552 at the Siege of Metz. Holy Roman Emperor Charles V was trying to take the city, but the French held out, and Charles suffered a humiliating defeat. The people burned an effigy of the emperor and a group of tanners created a grotesque version of the burned image, which morphed into Père Fouettard. Either or both of these origins are possible, but either way, he is another of the saint's helpers who acts as the enforcer to keep bad children in line.

Père Fouettard usually appears in a dark robe with wild hair and a dark beard, carrying a whip or a bundle of switches. He sometimes wears a dark hat and has a sack for carrying off especially bad children, or a basket to extra sticks and beating implements. He might also carry *les grelots* (the bells) to warn children that he is on the way. He's a kind of "anti-Santa," and his intentions are anything but amiable. If the kids are lucky, they'll only get a lump of coal from him. But according to old tales, whippings or even eviscerations were possible for especially bad children!

If Père Fouettard carries a whip, it is usually a martinet, a whip with a wooden handle and several leather thongs or lashes. It was used until the 1970s as a way of disciplining children both at home and in schools, an unpleasant reminder that abuse of children was considered completely acceptable in recent times in some surprising places. Of course, France still used the guillotine to execute criminals as late as 1977...

In the 1930s, an American version of this unsavory character appeared in the United States, known by the charming name "Father Flog" or "Spanky," and was sometimes accompanied by "Mother Flog." This odd character doesn't seem to have had much to do with Christmas, though, and was probably just another nasty invention to try to keep misbehaving children in line.

Hans Trapp

Alsace-Lorraine and France

Hans is another of those holiday fiends who brings not presents and joy, but punishment, pain, and even death in some circumstances.

Hans was based on a real German knight named Hans von Trotha, who lived in the second half of the fifteenth century. This historical Hans fell afoul of some local monks and the church, and was eventually excommunicated, though by the end of his life, he seems to have reconciled with the church, and the excommunication order was lifted after his death. Not so, according to legend. Hans was evil to the core, and delighted in committing foul deeds and living a debauched life. It was whispered that he'd made a pact with the devil, and even before his so-called death, he came to roam the forests of historical Alsace-Lorraine—modern-day eastern France and western Germany (though some legends place him in Bavaria in the south)—having lost his mind as a result of the evil deeds he'd committed.

Like all good fairy tales from that fertile region, children had the most to fear from him, for he was ever searching for them, eager to kill them and consume them to satisfy his hunger for human flesh. He dressed in rags stuffed with straw, which made him look like a homicidal scarecrow, and indeed, he used that disguise to capture unwary travelers. But more often, he sought out anyone who strayed too far into the woods, especially children. And so it was for many years, until God decided to punish him while he roasted a child, by striking him with lightning and splitting open his skull.

This seems to have been a temporary setback, however, for soon he was offered the chance to redeem himself by—you guessed it—accompanying St. Nicholas on his excursions to both reward and punish children according to their year's deeds. In some versions of the legend, Hans has repented his evil ways and now repays his debt to Nicholas by being his faithful servant, but in others, he's just as awful as he always was, and children cannot count on Nicholas's benevolence to save them from this demon if they've misbehaved! He's always on the lookout for the ones that he wants to eat on Christmas Eve, by the way.

Children would sometimes sing songs to him at the holidays, to explain how they've been good and he shouldn't come to them with any ill intent. No word on how well this worked, though.

Like so many of these weird Christmas monsters, the character of Hans is now a staple of holiday celebrations and pageants in Alsace and the surrounding areas, where the actor playing him often looks like a demonized version of Santa Claus. He might run up to children and scare them, but it's all in good fun. At least, we hope so!

Zwarte Piet

Belgium and the Netherlands

Zwarte Piet is problematic, to say the least. "Black Pete" is one of St. Nicholas's helpers and enforcers, as with so many other holiday monsters. But this version is different and even disturbing to modern sensibilities. Piet was usually portrayed as a Moor, someone of North African or even sub-Saharan African origin, who joined the saint to dispense punishment to children deserving of it, using a birch rod to whip them. But over the centuries, festivals that incorporated the character almost always included a white actor in blackface playing the role, with all of its caricatures and implications. Since the mid-1800s, actors playing the role have darkened their skin with makeup, applied lipstick, and worn large curly wigs, all to bizarrely emphasize his African origins, at least according to ugly stereotypes.

Recently, there has been a movement to downplay or remove Piet from Dutch and Belgian holiday pageants altogether, with accusations of racism and the use of colonial imagery being the most common reasons to do so. And it's easy to understand why. In this form, Piet is one of many problematic figures that date back to the colonial era, with the implications that non-Europeans were "savages" who had to be "tamed" by Europe and the United States. It would be better, modern objectors say, to remove the character altogether, or substitute another one in the same role.

There has been pushback, of course, from those who say that Piet is nothing more than a harmless tradition, that he's not intended to represent any person or any real people, and that Piet is as much a fantasy character as Krampus, or any of the other odd creations that haunt the winter landscape. The blackface itself was not taken from Africans, they argue, but rather from an older tradition of blackening the face to hide oneself from evil spirits, which is medieval in origin. And they do have a point here, but it also seems likely that the black-faced companion, which in the Middle Ages sometimes was shown as a demon in chains, was transformed into a Moor at the height of the European colonial age (1850-ish) to make a point about how the "demons" of the other continents had to be subdued.

Protests against Piet's racist imagery have been regular over the last decade or so, and in response, some festivals have substituted a new character, Roetveegpietm, or "Sooty Piet," whose "blackness" comes from soot smeared on his face. This character can thus be played by anyone of any ethnic background, and he still takes on the role of Nicholas's helper and companion and does all the same things as Piet. But not everyone is happy with this change, and arguments over the character and how he should appear have sometimes sunk into shouting matches, protests, and have even come to blows and property damage. Clearly, it's an issue with heated opinions.

Polls have shown that while a large majority of Dutch people think that Piet is an important part of their cultural heri-tage and should remain, a growing number are willing to see changes made (such as the soot) to bring him into the twenty-first century and keep his portrayal more in line with modern sensibilities. Time will tell how successful this attempt at change will be.

Grýla and Leppalúði

Iceland

Ah, nothing says "the holidays" like a good bit of old-fashioned cannibalism! And two of the most impressive cannibals in all of Iceland are Grýla and Leppalúði. Grýla is an ogress who was first mentioned way back in the thirteenth century (and might have been known in oral traditions even earlier), which means that she's been terrorizing Icelandic children for a long time! Similar ogres exist in the Faroe Islands and Ireland, though Grýla's association with the Christmas season only seems to date back to the seventeenth century.

Grýla is always hungry, always looking for fresh meat. And what is her favorite dish? Naughty child, of course! According to some old poems, Grýla disguises herself as a common beggar and asks parents if she can take their badly behaved children, presumably to correct them. Of course, her real intention is to take them back to her lair and devour them! She is said to have once lived in a village, but was driven away to a remote location, a cave in the lava fields of Dimmuborgir (a place that inspired the name of a massively popular Norwegian black metal band, incidentally).

She is said to be huge and repulsive in appearance, sporting multiple heads with eyes on the back of them, as well as a beard, a tail, and fangs (to be honest, the reports vary). She is sometimes accompanied by her husband, the troll named Leppalúði. He is actually her third mate; she ate the first, Gustr, and killed the second, Boli. Leppalúði doesn't seem to be as malevolent as her, so perhaps that's why she keeps him around. Their children are very important, for they are the famed Yule Lads (see the next entry, page 75), and their house pet is the dreaded Yule Cat (see page 78).

Perhaps due to the bitterness of Icelandic weather in December, she becomes especially hungry at the holidays, and is eager to seek out naughty children, shove them into her sack, and drag them back to cook up in a stew. Icelandic children were warned to be on their best behavior to avoid attracting her attention. And children were expected to behave well throughout the year, because Grýla knew if a child was good all year, or was just putting on an act during the holidays to avoid getting snapped up. Once again, parents seem to have devised an amusing but probably psychologically scarring way of getting their kids to behave themselves!

Leppalúði, on the other hand, doesn't seem to have much interest in going out and procuring children for the dinner table, content to stay at home in their cave. Maybe he doesn't like eating children, or maybe he's just lazy.

Some legends say that Grýla and Leppalúði died some time ago, because there simply weren't enough naughty children to keep them alive anymore, but that might just be wishful thinking.

The Thirteen Yule Lads

Iceland

The Yule Lads are the sons of Grýla and Leppalúði (though some traditions have them as Grýla's brothers) and, like them, the Lads started off as evil and nasty characters, but, unlike mom, they became somewhat nicer over the centuries. Maybe Grýla and Leppalúði had caused enough emotional damage to Icelandic children already? In fact, there was even an Icelandic law passed in the eighteenth century that prohibited parents from using stories of the ogres and Yule Lads to discipline and frighten their children into behaving. How this was enforced is anyone's guess.

In any case, the Lads came from a time when it was thought that evil spirits and malevolent forces descended from the mountains to prey upon mortals in the dark months of the year. These boys were always mischievous, but their appearances shifted from those of ugly ogres and trolls with ill intent into something more humanlike and jolly. According to legend, there were once as many as eighty-two of them (!), but over time many were combined together and reimagined down to their current thirteen, to represent the days before the arrival of Christmas. Some regions of Iceland believed in an even smaller number, such as nine. And one odd little song speaks of two female Yule Ladies, who liked to steal fat and hide it up their noses or in their socks. Nursery rhymes, eh?

By the end of the nineteenth, century, the Lads had taken on the role of multiple Santas, who would bring treats to houses in the villages. They were said to leave these treats in the shoes of children who had been good, but would leave rotten potatoes in the shoes of those who weren't, a unique spin on the lump of coal. By the 1930s, adults dressed as the Yule Lads were even visiting schools and radio stations, dressed in pseudomedieval Icelandic garb, or something akin to Santa suits. No cannibals here!

And yet, their names are reminders of their trouble-making past, even if they've been downgraded to pranksters from vicious child-eaters. One Lad would arrive on each night during the season:

December 12, Stekkjarstaur (Sheep-Cote Clod): He steals milk from sheep, but has one peg leg, so he makes a lot of noise.

December 13, Giljagaur (Gully Gawk): He loves milk from cows, but rather than stealing from their udders directly, he will wait for humans to milk them, and then take it.

December 14, Stúfur (Stubby): As the name implies, he's quite short, and likes to eat the leftover crusts on cooking pans. Ew.

December 15, Þvörusleikir (Spoon-Licker): Again, his name is his profession. He steals spoons to lick food off them. But he's emaciated because there is never enough food stuck to them.

December 16, Pottaskefill (Pot-Scraper): He likes to scrape leftover food from pots, and is presumably a little less scrawny than his brother!

December 17, Askasleikir (Bowl-Licker): We're seeing a pattern here! He sneaks out to lick clean any bowls with leftover food in them, even if they've been intended for dogs and cats. He will hide under beds and snatch the bowls away from the poor animals. Jerk.

December 18, Hurðaskellir (Door-Slammer): This one isn't interested in food; he just likes slamming doors to wake up people at night. We've all had neighbors like that...

December 19, Skyrgámur (Skyr-Gobbler): He loves skyr (a

kind of Icelandic cheese-yogurt), and will steal it if he can.

December 20, Bjúgnakrækir (Sausage-Swiper): This one likes to take the sausages that hang from the ceiling for smoking. He hides in the rafters and snatches them away.

December 21, Gluggagægir (Window-Peeper): He likes to look through windows to try to see what's going on and what he might be able to steal. Creep.

December 22, Gáttaþefur (Doorway-Sniffer): He uses his large nose to seek out *laufabrauð* ("leaf bread," a traditional Icelandic holiday Christmas pastry) from far away. At least he's not licking pet food bowls!

December 23, Ketkrókur (Meat-Hook): This guy is a little more aggressive and likes to carry around a meat hook to grab cuts of meat. Perhaps in earlier times, he used this to ensnare children.

December 24, Kertasníkir (Candle-Stealer): This weirdo likes to sneak up on children and steal their candles after they've gone to bed, not for the light, but so he can eat them. They were made from animal fat back in the old days, you see.

And those are the Yule Lads in a nutshell. While they can be a pain, at least they leave children something in return for the nuisance they cause!

Jólakötturinn, the Yule Cat

Iceland

The idea of a "Yule cat" might seem appealing at first: a soft, cuddly little feline to warm one on a chilly evening, and perhaps curl up in front of a cozy fire, purring and content. Or maybe he brings presents to good children, like so many other fantastical beings out there. But oh no, definitely not. The Jólakötturinn of Iceland is terrifying, but for what might seem really mundane reasons. First of all, this is no mere house cat. The Yule Cat is enormous in size and lies in wait in the dark to exact revenge on hapless children. What is their crime? Their clothing.

Yes, you see, an old folk custom in Iceland was that children who did all of their chores would receive new clothes for Christmas. Now, most children these days cringe at the thought of Christmas clothing. They dread receiving either socks and underwear (shudder), or some horrible holiday sweater that they will be forced to wear at the next family gathering, while shriveling up in embarrassment. But for children living in the harsh and cold climate of Iceland, new winter clothing would have been most welcome. And they were expected to wear new clothing on Christmas night. Why? Because the Yule Cat would come and check up on them.

Yes, this gigantic feline would creep into every farm and village on Christmas night and peer into each window to see what the children were wearing. If they'd been good, they would be adorned in their fabulous new Christmas digs, or have them at hand to show off. But if the children had been bad (i.e., they

haven't done all their chores) and didn't have at least one new item of clothing, the cat would do two things: first, eat whatever dinner was made for them. But going hungry was the least of their worries, for next, he would drag the naughty children out of their homes and eat them as the main course!

Written legends of the Yule Cat only date back to the nineteenth century, but the tradition is probably much older than that. The Norse goddess Freya was said to ride in a chariot drawn by two cats, and a number of other beings could shape-shift at will, so it's possible that belief in the monstrous cat originated in pagan times. But it might just as easily have been an invention of worn-out parents who needed the children to pull their own weight around the house. In addition, it seems to have become a tradition so that those who were better off would be mindful of those who were not. The poor might need the charity of some new (or at least new-to-them) clothing to stave off the dreadful fate of being snapped up by the ravenous monster cat lurking in the snowy wilds outside their dwellings. If you could avoid getting eaten, you were probably going to have a good year!

The Tomte

Scandinavia

The Tomte is a delightful Scandinavian elf-like being who, much like Santa, brings holiday happiness and joy to... oh, who are we kidding? He can be absolutely horrifying! He's not necessarily one for laughing and being cheerful, but tends to keep to himself and doesn't like to be bothered. His appearance can be, admittedly, rather comical. He might be seen as a small, old-looking man, wearing gray-colored rustic clothing and sporting a large pointed cap pulled down over his eyes, as well as a big, bushy beard. Or he might look completely different. That's because while there is only one Santa, there are many Tomtar (the plural). They live on farms and other homes in Scandinavia, and belief in them might be a holdover from a time when people believed in house and land spirits, with whom they had to cohabit and make peace with, if things were going to run smoothly. The spirits were there first, after all.

Tomte will usually choose either a corner of the barn, or perhaps a space under the floorboards or in the rafters, and they prefer to be left alone. Trying to get their attention or have them make an appearance in one's home will likely just annoy them. If you treat them well, they will respond in kind, but if you get on their bad side, watch out! A happy Tomte will clean your house and your barn, while an offended one might ruin your crops, steal your possessions, or even make your cows grow sick and die. Clearly, they are not beings to trifle with.

So what does all of this have to do with Christmas, you might be asking? Well, during that special and happy time of year, it's expected that the homeowner will leave out a bowl of porridge topped with a pat of butter. Do this, and your Tomte

will be very grateful. Neglect to do it, and he might well kill you in your sleep! There are legends and folktales about what happens if the porridge is not left out. In one case, a farmer's daughter decided to eat the Tomte's porridge, instead of making it an offering. The offended creature began to sing, and she was compelled to dance. But she couldn't stop, and in the end she danced herself to death. In another tale, a grumpy blacksmith decides he'd rather have the porridge himself. He not only eats it, but then he takes a poop in the bowl to add insult to injury! The outraged Tomte devised a terrible punishment. A few days later, when the blacksmith was at his forge, the creature pushed him into the flames and allowed him to be burned up completely, except for his feet, which the Tomte left on the floor, still in their shoes. Happy holidays!

Another story tells of an offended Tomte killing a farmer's cow in anger because the butter was left off the porridge, only to discover that it was at the bottom of the bowl the whole time. Regretting his mistake, he steals a cow from a neighboring farm to replace the one he killed. Nice, huh?

In any case, if the family did the right thing on Christmas Eve, and woke up the next day to find that the bowl was empty, it usually meant that the Tomte was pleased and that they would have good fortune for another year. So forget milk and cookies for Santa; leave out that steaming bowl of porridge—your life might depend on it!

Is Santa Claus Actually Odin?

Scandinavia

You might have heard this question asked from time to time, or seen articles about it pop up during the holidays. So, did the mighty Allfather of Norse mythology, the bloody one-eyed god of battle and death, really become jolly old Santa in his red suit? The short answer is no. The long answer is a little bit more complex.

There are some superficial similarities, such as the long beard, the snowy northern landscapes, using a flying animal to get around, and...well, that's about it, really. And yet, you'll still see new articles posted each year about how the Norse god is really the jolly old elf (and yes, some people do believe that Santa himself is an elf because of a line in the original Clement Clarke Moore poem—that's another conversation entirely). To be fair, elves do come from Norse pagan beliefs. Known as the *alfr* (*alf* is singular), they were said to be shining beings of light who dwelled in their own realm and sometimes functioned as go-betweens for the gods and humanity, perhaps a little bit like angels. In addition to these "light" elves, there were also "dark" elves, and possibly "swart elves," that came to be known as dwarves.

Now, the dwarves were masters of crafting and smithing, so the idea of a bearded old man having elves make toys for him does seem possible. But it's really nothing more than a coincidence. The first mention of elves working for Santa seems to be from the short story "Christmas Elves" by Louisa May Alcott (of *Little Women* fame), written in 1855. No matter what anyone tells you, there is nothing connecting Odin to bringing gifts to Norse children at Yuletide except wishful thinking.

But what about his eight-legged horse, Sleipnir? Odin rides this magnificent beast through the sky and through different worlds, right? Yes, he does. But that doesn't connect him to a sleigh pulled by eight reindeer. The eight-legged horse is found in Central Asian beliefs, and the animal that a shaman can mount to ride through different worlds comes from Siberia. The reindeer as we know them first appeared in a pamphlet from 1821, with the rather bulky title of *A New Year's Present, to the Little Ones from Five to Twelve Number III: The Children's Friend.*

Some have argued that since Santa as we know him comes from Father Christmas, Father Christmas must come from Odin. But this is really not the case.

If anything, a more likely candidate would be the Norse god Thor, who traveled in a sled pulled by two goats. Father Christmas was invented—probably in the seventeenth century—as a kind of German Protestant reaction to the Catholic veneration of St. Nicholas, the original "St. Nick" who, as we've seen, did indeed bring gifts to people (though he often tried to keep it quiet). These Protestants liked the idea of Nicholas, but wanted to take away the Catholic connections. The English also adopted the idea of Father Christmas, who was a holiday tradition by the nineteenth century. Nicholas survived in Catholic areas of Germany, accompanied by Krampus and a host of other horrors.

And, of course, the Netherlands preserved the idea of St. Nicholas and continued to use him as the main holiday gift giver, soon to be known as Sinterklaas, from which we get Santa Claus. So, sorry to say, the great god of the Vikings has little or nothing to do with our beloved gift giver!

Is Santa Claus a Shaman?

Polar Regions

Okay, so you might have also heard this one. Is Santa Claus based in any way on the shamans of Siberia and the north? This might seem like a very odd question, but some who have studied the figure do see some fascinating similarities. But first, we should begin by discussing the word "shaman." It has become a generic term for the spiritual practices of almost any indigenous people anywhere in the world, but this is a bit lazy and incorrect. Properly, a shaman is one of the holy people of the cultures of Siberia, and their practices are not exactly the same as those found elsewhere. As such, there has been a move to reclaim the term and use it only in connection with those people who originated it, which seems fair.

An alternative term is animism, which can be used to describe the spiritual workings of any number of native peoples around the world. And with that established, we can talk about the Sámi, the indigenous people of Sápmi, the lands of northern Norway, Sweden, Finland, and Western Russia (incorrectly known as Lapland). They have a number of interesting cultural traditions that bear an almost creepy resemblance to our stories of Santa.

In some Sámi settlements, people traditionally would be visited by their holy persons at the solstice or other times. They would come to perform spiritual and healing work, often while using the hallucinogenic mushroom *Amanita muscaria*, also known as fly agaric, which is a red toadstool with white spots. The holy persons would often imitate this mushroom by dressing in red and white.

Old Sámi dwellings resembled tepees, and if they were covered in show, the holy person might have to enter from the top, i.e., where the smoke from fires escapes.

These holy ones would bring the gifts of healing and messages from beyond, and afterward they would be thanked with gifts of food in return.

They would then leave, often on sleds pulled by animals, especially, yes, reindeer. And reindeer, by the way, enjoy nibbling on fly agaric mushrooms and will seek them out.

It's also worth mentioning that northern Finland is still touted by Finnish tourist organizations as the "home of Santa Claus."

None of this proves that Sámi or even Siberian traditions are the origin of some of our most famous ideas about Santa, of course, but some have suggested that Clement Clarke Moore, who is credited with writing the 1823 poem "A Visit from St. Nicholas," better known as "'Twas the Night Before Christmas," might have been drawing upon old northern legends and descriptions of ancient traditions that were just beginning to make their way into greater awareness at the time.

This doesn't mean that there is a direct connection between magic mushrooms and Santa, but rather that our ideas about Santa are formed from several influences. One of them might well be the healers of the snowy north, who visited people via reindeer in the coldest time of the year to bring healing and health, and who dressed in the bright red of their most useful tool.

So, could Santa be enjoying the hallucinogenic power of these mushrooms every December 24th? Who knows?

Nuuttipukki and Joulupukki

Finland

There are many different versions of Santa, Father Christmas, St. Nicholas, and other winter gift bringers from the folklore of northern nations and cultures. The American Santa Claus came from the Dutch Sinterklass, and it was a Finnish American artist, Haddon Sundblom, who created the iconic image of Santa for Coca-Cola ads in the 1930s. This is the Santa that Americans know today, though similar versions had already existed for decades.

And yet, in Sundbolm's native Finland, there was another gift giver, one who might have a darker past: Joulupukki. The word means "Yule Goat," and might hint at the figure's ancient, even pagan, origins. As we've seen, the Norse god Thor traveled in a chariot drawn by two goats, and this might have provided at least a kernel of an idea for later versions of a winter figure who visited mortal homes at Yule (which was not the same as the winter solstice, but often fell in early January). The Yule Goat is still a treasured holiday tradition in Scandinavia, where little straw versions of the creature are put up with the other holiday decorations, and giant ones are set up, especially the famed goat at Gävle in Sweden, usually in the hopes that they won't be burned down by vandals before the end of the holidays.

It's thought that some rituals might have involved participants wearing goats' horns, though this is by no means certain. Over time, it seems that some pranksters, especially in Finnish lands, began to dress up in horns and go from home to home,

threatening mischief and mayhem unless they received gifts or food. Known as the Nuuttipukki, they were based on evil spirits that would torment mortals, presumably for the fun of it. As with some of the other examples we've seen, this demand for treats seems related to Halloween trick-or-treating and Celtic celebrations of Samhain in some way, but it might be simply that the same idea evolved in more than one place over time.

So the Joulupukki, in the form of a fearsome and nightmarish goat, might have been found in the company of the Nuuttipukki, bringing potential dread to the houses of superstitious country folk for centuries. Later, it was a kind of extortion racket: give us treats and we'll leave you alone. But by the nineteenth century, Joulupukki seems to have morphed into a nicer, more Santa-like figure, bringing gifts for children. The tradition continues today, as someone dressed up as Joulupukki will knock at the door (rather than climbing down a chimney) to ask if there are any good and well-behaved children at the house. It's all very similar to St. Nicholas in the Germanic countries.

The Nuuttipukki still make an appearance in some regions of Finland on January 13, Nuutinpäivä, or St. Knut's Day (and closer to the time when the Vikings celebrated Yule), sometimes known as the "twentieth day of Christmas." Hey, why not keep a good thing going? Revelers wander from home to home, dressed in their scary masks and horns, and demand holiday cheer, most often leftover alcohol. And so, a tradition that might have originated as a very real fear of the denizens of the winter dark continues as a fun, if sometimes obnoxious, folk custom.

The Hiding of the Brooms

Norway

Norway is a vast, beautiful country filled with stunning wilderness, majestic fjords, and, apparently, a lot of evil spirits and malevolent witches. And these creatures of the night like nothing better than to come out on Christmas Eve to cause no end of trouble. So what can a traditionally superstitious and vulnerable Norwegian do for protection? The answer is really simple: hide all of the household brooms in closets, where said witches and spirits can't find them. If you don't do this, they will enter your house, steal the brooms, and ride about in the night, doing evil and probably ruining Christmas for everyone.

Some people in Norway still practice this ancient custom, mainly for fun these days. What could be better than scaring your children with tales of malicious creatures invading your house and taking things, on the very night when benevolent old Father Christmas (or some equivalent) is set to appear and give our presents?

Of course, if you have a lot of cleaning to do on the night before Christmas, you should probably get on with it sooner rather than later, and remember to put all your brooms away before turning in. Better yet, just save the work until December 26. Mops and feather dusters are probably okay to leave out; a witch riding a mop would just look ridiculous.

This curious custom probably has a number of origin stories, and might even date back to pagan times. While spirits riding brooms were not a legend of the Viking Age, the idea of evil spirits all around certainly was. The good spirits of the land also had to be honored and placated, lest they turn against, say, the owner of a farm and cause troubles of their own.

While witches were not necessarily regarded as evil, there were both women known as *völva* ("wise woman") and practitioners of a kind of magic known as *seidr*, which was associated with the goddess Freya. The women (and sometimes men) who practiced it were often viewed with suspicion, and might have lived apart from the community, only to be consulted for help when they were needed. They didn't ride brooms, but they might carry an iron wand or some other implement that was a focus for their power. Freya herself was not an evil goddess at all, and was widely worshipped and adored. After the coming of Christianity, though, she was thrown under the proverbial bus like the other Norse gods and demonized, so the idea of wise women or "witches" being servants of evil (i.e., Freya) probably took hold, or was at least forced on local populations.

With the rise of the European witch-hunting crazes from the fifteenth to the seventeenth centuries, ideas about witches took on more solid form, including the notion that they rode around on broomsticks in service of the devil. And what better night to cause harm than on the eve of the holiest day in the Christian year? So, it was imperative that all good folk hide away their brooms to stop as much evil as possible before the arrival of Christmas Day. It was also a good excuse not to clean for a bit.

Lussi

Scandinavia

Scandinavia has a long-honored tradition of celebrating St. Lucia on December 13. Lucia was a saint said to have died in the early fourth century. According to legend, she was a martyr for refusing to renounce her Christian faith, and yet she could not be killed when the Romans tried to burn her, so they stabbed her to death instead. She became a popular saint in post-pagan Scandinavia, with legends of her piety and of her wearing a wreath on her head that held candles. She did this to keep her arms free when bringing food to Christians in hiding in the catacombs beneath Rome. Lucia celebrations in modern Scandinavia still feature girls wearing candle-crowns, which require a bit of skill and balance to keep even. She is one of the very few Catholic saints still honored in these Protestant countries. In Norse mythology, the sun is a goddess, Sol, or Sunna, who is forever chased by a wolf that tries to devour her light, so the idea of a feminine divine figure as a light-bringer is very old.

The beloved northern tradition of Lucia has a darker side, though, in the form of an evil witch named Lussi. It's possible that she was created out of a confusion between Lucia and Lucifer, but, however it happened, Lussi was decidedly less nice to the people on that same night of December 13. She developed into a witch or evil sorceress who might have accompanied the Wild Hunt (page 53) on its harvest of souls. The spirits that attend her and follow her are called the Lussiferda, which again, might be a play on Lucifer.

So December 13 is not only a night for St. Lucia, it is also sometimes called Lussinatta or "Lussi Night," a time when she roams the world, searching for wayward mortals to be snatched up and made to join the Wild Hunt, never to see their homes or loved ones again. Spirits, trolls, bad elves, and others go with her, and people are advised to take care if they must be outside that night. Naughty children are especially vulnerable. But it's not enough just to hide inside. If a child has been especially bad, Lussi might force her way down the chimney to abduct him or her. And it gets even worse: Lussi and her minions can invade your dreams, and might even take you from them. So if at all possible, it's a good idea to stay up until dawn (and away from the chimney) to make sure that you're safe!

Adults shouldn't think that they're getting off easily here. Lussi knows if you've not finished all those boring household chores. Traditionally, this would have been things like preparing storage for winter, salting and smoking meat, winterizing the home, and so on. Even parents needed to be on their best and most responsible behavior. If these tasks were left undone, Lussi might press her fearsome face to the window and scream at them, or even attack the house and try to tear down the chimney to get in.

In recent times, the practice of being awake all night, known as *Lussevaka*, has become an excuse to stay up and celebrate until dawn. While it might be a good reason for an all-night party now, the tradition clearly has a darker and more sinister origin. On the night of December 13, Lussi just might be coming for you, so watch out!

Mummers

Across Europe and Elsewhere

Mummers and mumming have a long tradition in many European countries, as well as in America. The practice isn't all that different from modern trick-or-treating at Halloween, but it's done at the December holidays instead. A long-standing European medieval tradition, it involved people donning costumes and weird masks, and going door-to-door to sing, dance, or perform in some other way, as we've seen in many of the previous entries. In return, they were expected to be rewarded with a small amount of food and drink. If this sounds like extortion, it pretty much is, but the theory is that everyone is caught up in the fun and goes along with it. It's rather like caroling groups going door-to-door, but with a somewhat creepier twist.

People's enjoyment of costumed revels dates back further than the Middle Ages, to Greece, and possibly even ancient Egypt. It's thought that the word "mumming" derives from the Greek *momus*, a representation of satire. Mimes also come from this word and its traditions (for better or worse!), and probably also the phrase "to keep mum," indicating that one didn't want to give away one's identity from behind the mask. Indeed, early mummers are said have made their way through the streets and into homes at certain festivals without saying anything, much less singing or dancing. They simply hid behind their masks and expected food or drink, which wouldn't have been creepy, no, not at all!

Mumming was especially popular in medieval Britain and Ireland, and, over time, plays were created with stock characters and plots that were performed every year. Though most

often associated with Christmas, there were celebrations at other times of the year, too, such as Easter. Mummer plays were something that people looked forward to as part of their celebrations. They were frowned upon during the Protestant Reformation, but continued on in some regions and in countries that remained Catholic. In recent decades, they've been revived by many folklore groups and are once again an important part of seasonal celebrations.

Indeed, modern versions of mumming continue in several countries, such as Latvia, where winter holiday revelers dress up as animals or sometimes as darker, creepier, demon-like beasties and put on garish masks. They go throughout neighborhoods in the time-honored manner, singing and making merry to drive out evil spirits. And, like their medieval counterparts, they expect some rewards for their efforts. They will often hide not only their faces, but also their voices to disguise their identities, and this means that someone answering the door will have no idea who they are. Imagine finding out your boss was out there dressed as a demon and was demanding chocolate or wine from you!

Another modern celebration, the Philadelphia Mummers Parade, keeps the tradition alive in the United States, with an annual parade on New Year's Day filled with colorful characters and up to 15,000 participants. It's been going on since 1900, and shows no signs of stopping. Mumming is alive and well, colorful, a bit weird, kind of creepy, and a whole lot of fun!

La Befana

Italy

Among scary Christmas and holiday figures, the Christmas witch Befana isn't as frightening as you might think. She brings gifts for good children on Epiphany Eve (January 5), leaving candies and other presents in their stockings if they have behaved, or lumps of coal and sticks if they haven't. Or sometimes, the children get garlic or onions; at least they don't get eaten alive! If the family leaves out a small glass of wine and some bites to eat, she might even sweep up the house a little before leaving, though after a few too many glasses between all the houses, she probably wouldn't do a very good job of tidying up.

Her name probably derives from "epiphany," and she has been a staple of Italian holiday celebrations for a long time. Some have suggested that she is actually connected to Strenua, goddess of the new year and the promise it brings.

La Befana is described as looking like an old hag in a black hood, who rides a broom and has soot on her face from dropping down so many chimneys. But you're not supposed to catch sight of her, or she will give you a thump on the head or shoulders with her broom, a good way to keep anxious children in their beds that night.

There are various legends about her origin. One says that the magi, who had come to honor Jesus, asked her where the infant Jesus was, but she didn't know. Instead, she offered them lodgings for the night, and the next day they offered to let her join them. But she declined, since she had work to do. She soon changed her mind and decided to set out to find the baby,

but was never able to, and so she still roams the world, looking for the child she never got to see, and leaving presents for all children.

A less happy version of the tale says that she had a baby of her own, but tragedy struck and the child died. She was overcome with grief and set out wandering when she heard of Jesus's birth. Thinking in her madness that the child was hers, she tried desperately to find him. When she did, she brought gifts to him, and, in return, she was made the "mother" of all Italian children.

Still another grim version states that she turned away the magi because she was too busy with her chores, but feeling guilty about it, she went after them. She brought gifts and a broom for Mary, but wasn't able to find the baby Jesus, so she now wanders the world forever, looking for a child that she will never find. She leaves gifts at every home, hopeful that one day she will complete her quest.

Befana is a mainstay of public celebrations of the day, where many actors will dress up as her. Often children receive "lumps of coal" as gifts, which are really pieces of rock candy colored black, a fun continuation of an old tradition. And it might imply that they've been a bit naughty in the previous year, but not too much...

Saturnalia

Ancient Rome

As the name implies, Saturnalia honored the god Saturn. It was a wild and crazy festival that took place in the middle of December (usually the 17th to the 23rd), corresponding pretty closely to the later Christmas holidays. It would begin solemnly enough, with a ceremony in honor of the ancient god, and thereafter, the celebrants held a banquet that was open to all. This was a gathering of feasting and also of drinking, and alcohol featured heavily in the festivities. We have accounts of people getting rip-roaring drunk in public, something that was normally forbidden. Undoubtedly, things did get out of hand, and fights certainly broke out among the intoxicated. Still, drunkenness seems to have been expected if one was truly going to have a good time.

In fact, many of the standard accepted behaviors of the time were overturned during that raucous week. Gambling in public was rife, even though this was normally prohibited. Indeed, gambling for money was still technically illegal, so sometimes gamblers would use nuts or other objects instead, but who knows how much this law was really enforced? Dress codes were relaxed, and even slaves were permitted to wear clothing that was normally forbidden to them, including a cone-shaped "freedman's cap," a hat that normally only freed slaves were allowed to wear. It's said that even Roman emperors put these on their heads from time to time. Slaves were also permitted to join the feasting and have a degree of freedom they usually wouldn't have, and could even disobey and talk back to their masters without fear of punishment.

The whole week was about role reversals and overturning norms, and many houses would appoint from among the servants a "lord" to rule over them for the week. This temporary tyrant could give all sorts of absurd orders to the household, such as that others must trade insults, get naked and dance, or whatever else came to mind. The sillier, the better.

People of all social classes exchanged gifts at the time, and these could be anything from serious to ridiculous, frugal to extravagant. There were even "secret Santa" type parties where everyone would bring gifts that were then randomly given to all participants. Some attendees received expensive items, while others received junk or jokes, but everyone was expected to accept their presents with good humor.

This topsy-turvy tradition continued into the Middle Ages in Europe, when, during the Christmas holidays, servants and working-class people would appoint a "Lord of Misrule" to engage in absurd activities. Even in the ecclesiastical world, a young chorister or other member of the church would often be appointed as the "Boy Bishop," and have power over his elders and seniors, at least for a day or two. Church officials sometimes frowned on these activities because of their pagan origins and disrespect for authority, but many officials saw them as a needed blowing off of steam, especially for younger people. These practices of Christmas chaos continued in Britain and elsewhere until the Reformation. People needed a way to get through the dark days of early winter, whether pagan or pseudo-Christian, and the absurd revelries of a world temporarily turned on its head were just the thing.

The Kallikantzari

The Balkans and Turkey

Unlike the previous two entries, the Kallikantzari or Kallikantzaroi are truly terrifying! They only show up for the twelve days of the Christmas season, but they can be anything from a nuisance to downright dangerous. Their appearance varies. In some accounts, they are obviously related to the satyrs of Greek myth, being half-man and half-goat. But they can also take on other forms: having boar tusks, red eyes, long tongues, horse's hooves, long tails, and dozens of other strange and scary features. They also like to gnaw on worms, snakes, and other ground-dwelling creatures as snacks. Some say they are huge, but more often they are described as are rather small, though that doesn't take away from their capacity for mischief and evil.

They are known by different names in different regions. In Serbia, the Karakondžula lie in wait during the nights of Christmas, hoping to attack those who stray outside. It was better to remain home and safe. In Bulgaria, the Karakondjul likewise hide in the dark, hoping to catch the unwary. In Albania, the horrific Kukuth are actually reanimated corpses that prowl in the dark nights of early January, laden with chains and said to have a breath that can kill. In Turkey, the Karakoncolos of Anatolia are described as being hairy and menacing (see page 110).

In holiday folklore, the Kallikantzari were known for trying to break into houses and then destroy everything inside. They might crawl down chimneys, sneak through keyholes (a very tight fit, that!), or enter through back doors. They would then cause damage, steal food, and, if they were lucky, try to steal

children, too, especially ones who were born on Christmas Day. Ways to thwart them included making sure that everything in the house was secure, scattering flour on the ground to track their uneven footprints, and burning a Yule log in the fireplace all night (to prevent them from coming through the chimney). Even better was to burn old shoes in the fireplace—the stench would keep them away! Another tactic was to put sweets in various places inside and outside the house, to tempt them into leaving everything else alone. Some traditions recommend putting sausages and donut-like pastries out on the roof. If the Kallikantzari love one thing more than worms and snakes, it's sugar!

These creatures could make life hell for people during the Christmas season, and the only respite was the coming of dawn, for they can't stand sunlight. And yet, that might not be enough to guarantee protection, for some legends suggest that anyone born during the twelve days of Christmas might be at risk of transforming into a Kallikantzari when they become adults. In order to prevent this, a baby born during this time was to be bound up with garlic and have their toenails singed. Seriously.

In folklore, the Kallikantzari aren't especially bright, which might also afford everyone some protection from their antics, but overall, they are everything from a pain in the butt to a genuine threat during the holidays, and all care needs to be taken in order to ensure that one's house isn't trashed!

Bocuk and Bocuk Night

Thrace and Turkey

In Thrace in western Turkey, in the village of Çamlıca, there is a tradition on January 6 that probably dates back to the Middle Ages known as Bocuk Night. On this night, locals enjoy dressing up in white sheets and robes and painting their faces in white and back—the creepier and more garish looking, the better. They then process though town with torches, knocking on doors and making a ruckus. As with a number of these winter festivals, it's all rather like a Halloween celebration a few months late. They are dressing up as the evil spirits that wander their region that night.

"Bocuk" refers to the coldest day of the year, and is a time when restless sprits and even malevolent witches are released to wander the earth, seeking to do harm. There are several versions of these entities: the Bocuk wife (*Bocuk karısı*), the Bocuk mother (*Bocuk anası*), and the Bocuk grandfather (*Bocuk dedesi*). Once freed, they will roam about, often attracted by barns, where they will enter and try to suck milk from cows that have just given birth, thus depriving their calves of needed nourishment. Even worse, if these witches succeed in doing this, the cow will no longer give milk.

The best way to prevent them from hurting anyone is to leave out a dessert made of baked pumpkin, which will distract them; traditionally, people left it in barns to lure the witches away from their cows. It's also important to eat enough of it oneself. Otherwise, it's not just animals that are in danger; any unfed person also risks being caught out by one of these entities, which will attach itself to their back and pull them down into the snow to a freezing death.

It all sounds pretty grim, but during the festival the dress-up is all in good fun and participants like to run around warning people: "Bocuk is coming!" It's essential that the people meet up around warm fires and share the pumpkin dessert, other homemade foods, and each other's company on this night, a gathering called Sedenka. The goodwill that this meeting generates will be enough to defeat the evil that stalks them at the edge of their villages and towns. Coming together as a community keeps these evil forces at bay and ensures that people's animals and crops will produce abundant food, and that the year ahead will be prosperous.

They will know they've succeeded in driving away evil and bringing forth a good year by placing water on a piece of wood and leaving it outside. If it's frozen by morning, the village will enjoy a good year and the forces of evil will have been defeated once again.

The Karakoncolos

Turkey

These creatures from Turkish folklore are dark, hairy, and frightening, like a Turkish Krampus. They appear most often during the first ten days of Zemheri, a time between December 22 and January 21, which in Turkey is the coldest time of the year.

They are obviously related to the Kallikantzari (page 105), but with some important differences. They are usually thought of as taller than other versions of these holiday pests, they are covered in hair that is thick and dark, and they don't seem to be as dim-witted or easily placated as their Balkan cousins. They also revel in deception, riddles, and mind games, all with the intent of doing harm.

They will sometimes lie in wait at night in dark corners of towns and villages, and ask passersby questions or give them riddles to solve. If the individual gives the wrong answer, then they risk being killed, rather like the Sphinx of ancient Greek myth. And there's an important detail: one's answer has to contain the word "black," and the creature might ask multiple questions before the person is free to go. If the individual messes up even once, they will likely be struck dead and the Karakoncolos will move on to find another victim.

These creatures are also known for being deceptive in other ways. One of the most notorious is to lie in wait outside of someone's home and call out to its inhabitant in the voice of a friend or family member. If the homeowner opens the door to answer, the Karakoncolos will lure them out and place the unfortunate person into a hypnotized trance. Once they've

done this, they will leave the victim out in the elements. In the cold and sometimes the snowy winters of central Turkey, this could be a death sentence. So people must be very careful about answering their doors in winter, unless they are sure of who is really there.

A related mystery monster, the Germakoçi, or "mountain man," is said to stalk the Laz region in northern Turkey, near the Black Sea. Like the Karakoncolos, it is tall, covered with hair, and dwells in the mountains and hills. Legends of this monster extend to nearby Georgia, where he is said to be a truly evil cannibal.

Both of these winter monsters bear a rather striking resemblance to Bigfoot and Yeti, in that they are tall, hairy, and inhabit remote regions. But whereas researchers in cryptozoology tend to think of those more famous unknowns as indifferent animals, these Turkish mysteries seem to be genuinely evil at heart, and take delight in causing harm during the winter months.

Good King Wenceslas Looked Down...and was Stabbed and Impaled

The Czech Republic

Everyone knows the jaunty little Christmas carol about how good King Wenceslas looked down on the Feast of Stephen (that's December 26, by the way), with its crisp and even snow and the important reminder to help those less fortunate. It's all sweet and wintery, even though the music was originally written for a spring-time song, but that's another story. But it was Wenceslas himself who was destined to be less fortunate.

He was born in about 907 in Bohemia (what is now the Czech Republic). His grandmother, Ludmilla, was a Christian, while his mother, Drahomira, was not. His father, Duke Vratislaus, died when he was about thirteen years old, leaving Ludmilla as regent for the kingdom until he came of age. Drahomira wasn't happy about this, and when Ludmilla was strangled sometime afterward, Drahomira was conveniently able to assume the regency on her son's behalf.

Wenceslas eventually became duke in his own right and sent his mother into exile. Having been influenced by his Christian grandmother, Wenceslas took a vow of virginity and wanted to convert all of Bohemia to Christianity. This effort didn't sit well with a lot of people, especially when he encouraged Christian missionaries from Germany to come in and begin preaching. After a German invasion of Bohemia, Wenceslas swore allegiance to its ruler, the Christian Henry I, and submitted to him. He probably saw advantages to allying with a powerful

monarch, but that infuriated many of his courtiers and peers, some of whom were sympathetic to his exiled mother. In particular, his own younger brother, the wonderfully named Boleslav the Cruel, began to plot treachery and murder.

On September 28, 935, the young Wenceslas was on his way to mass, when some of Boleslav's henchmen confronted him. They attacked him and stabbed him multiple times. Then Boleslav arrived and ran his brother through with a lance. In some versions of the tale, Wenceslas was dismembered after his death as a further sign of rebellion and humiliation. Of course, other Christians soon hailed the young man as a martyr, and various written versions of his short life and violent death circulated in the decades after his murder.

He and Ludmilla were soon venerated as saints, and the Holy Roman emperor Otto the Great (912–73) declared that Wenceslas deserved the title of "king" for his piety, which is why Wenceslas is now known as King Wenceslas, even though he was only a duke. His death is still commemorated in the Czech Republic on September 28, but it's his association with the holiday season that gives him worldwide fame, not his bloody and untimely end.

Caga Tió

Catalonia

Not so much scary, but more confusing, Caga Tió is a curious (to say the least) little character in Catalan Christmas celebrations. Caga Tió means "the pooping log," which gives you an idea of where this entry is going. It's also called Tió de Nadal, or "the Christmas log," a more socially acceptable name, but everyone who knows about it understands what one is really talking about.

Basically, Caga Tió is a small wooden log with a smiley face painted on one side, often propped up by two sticks on the face side. The back half is covered with a cloth. Starting with the Feast of the Immaculate Conception on December 8, children are expected to "feed" the log small bits of food, such as fruits and nuts, which are usually gone in the morning, if the parents have done their job! They continue to feed Caga Tió throughout the season, until the magic night of Christmas Eve arrives. And then, something very special (and scatological) happens.

The children leave the room for a while and pray for gifts, and often warm small sticks by the fire or heater. When they come back, they gather around Caga Tió again and sing songs to it (there are several traditional ones to choose from). While singing, they gently beat the log with their small sticks. This is presumably to help the log with its constipation, because at some point, the cloth is lifted and there, at its backside, Caga Tió will have "pooped" out treats for the children, secretly left under the cloth while the children were out of the room, of course! The most common treat is a type of nougat called turrón. Indeed, there are even versions of a song that the kids sing to make sure that they get the good stuff:

"Poop, tió, hazelnuts and nougats, pee white wine,

do not poop herrings, they are too salty,

poop nougats, they taste better.

Poop, tió, almonds and nougats,

and if you don't want to poop

I will hit you with a stick!

Poop, tió!"

This seems reasonable. After all, if your log is going to poop, it had better be something other than salty herrings!

So where did this decidedly unusual tradition originate? Honestly, no one really knows. *Turrón* has long been a holiday treat in Iberia, and might even have been brought to the region by the Moors in the Middle Ages. The log is probably one of those ubiquitous pagan rites that survived into modern times. The act of bringing home a log of wood might have symbolized a relationship to the natural world, and perhaps it was burned on select days or occasions. "Caring" for it with a blanket and food might have further symbolized that connection to the natural order of things. But as to when the log started pooping goodies? That's a mystery, even to the Catalan people, and maybe it's just as well.

Winter Werewolves

Pan-European

Ah, nothing says Christmas like werewolves! What could be more festive than transforming by the light of the full moon into a bloodthirsty beast that mindlessly brings death and misery to local populations of snowbound villages in the darkest time of the year? It has to be worth at least few carols, right? So, how on earth did werewolves get associated with the holidays?

Wolves were highly feared winter predators, of course, and while they don't attack humans (despite all of those movies and TV shows you've seen), they could take livestock and cause many other problems. So the idea that someone might deliberately turn into a wolf (or at least have no control over their transformation) was a fear that haunted the minds of many in Europe and beyond for centuries. In some areas, it was dangerous to even say the word "wolf" between Christmas and Epiphany, because people were afraid that doing so would summon them, or rather their lycanthropic counterparts. Many people believed it was better never to say the word "wolf" in December at all, just to be sure.

To make matters worse, traditional folk belief in Germany, Italy, and Romania held that if one was unfortunate enough to be born on Christmas Day (especially at the stroke of midnight), one was at a far higher risk of becoming a werewolf, because that day was set aside for Christ alone, and no one else should be born then. Not that this is something an individual can control, of course, but it might have also tied in with a belief that abstinence was preferred at Easter time in the spring. The night of St. Lucy (December 13) was thought to

be an especially likely time for werewolves to appear, whether there was a full moon or not.

Werewolves showed up throughout Europe at this time of year, and they had their own appalling celebrations. In 1555, the Swedish cleric Olaus Magnus (translated here by Anglican priest Sabine Baring-Gould) wrote that in areas such as Lithuania and Prussia:

"On the feast of the Nativity of Christ, at night, such a multitude of wolves transformed from men gather together in a certain spot, arranged among themselves, and then spread to rage with wondrous ferocity against human beings, and those animals which are not wild, that the natives of these regions suffer more detriment from these, than they do from true and natural wolves; for when a human habitation has been detected by them isolated in the woods, they besiege it with atrocity, striving to break in the doors, and in the event of their doing so, they devour all the human beings, and every animal which is found within. They burst into the beer-cellars, and there they empty the tuns of beer or mead, and pile up the empty casks one above another in the middle of the cellar, thus showing their difference from natural and genuine wolves."

Drunk werewolves? That makes the whole situation even worse!

There was also a late medieval Baltic legend about a boy with a lame leg who would summon the devil's followers to a general holiday meeting, which was not optional, by the way. Anyone who refused or was slow to respond would be lashed with an iron whip to get them there. At said gathering, everyone transformed into wolves and then went off to commit mayhem, presumably to ruin the holidays for everyone else.

Yeah, Christmas werewolves were once a big deal.

Christmas Spiders

Ukraine

Ah, spiders at Christmas! What could be more festive? If your arachnophobia is already getting stirred up, you might want to give this entry a miss, but it's really not as creepy as it sounds! In Ukraine, there is a tradition of spiders weaving webs at Christmas, so many people decorate their Christmas trees with at least one spiderweb ornament. Despite the terrifying potential that such an image brings, it's actually a rather sweet custom.

There's an old Ukrainian folktale about how it all started:

Once upon a time, there was a widow who was very poor and lived in a small home with her children. Outside, there grew a pine tree, and one day, a pine cone dropped from it and fell to the ground. Not long after, the cone began to grow a new tree. The widow's children were happy about this, because they thought that it might make a good Christmas tree when the time came, so they helped it grow tall enough to be a proper size for their tiny house.

As Christmas approached, they brought it inside, but there was a problem. Since they were so poor, they had no decorations to place on it, and they were saddened knowing that they would wake up to a bare tree on Christmas Day. The children started to cry and went to bed, sobbing, their tears continuing well into the night. Now, the home was old and naturally had resident spiders. These creatures heard the children's cries and decided to do something about it.

They crept out, went to the tree, and climbed up into it. Once there, they began to spin webs in beautiful patterns and

shapes, decorating the tree as if with ornaments. When the children woke up the next morning, they were shocked and delighted to see that their tree had been decorated by their little spider friends. They called to their mother to come and see the wonder before them. She was as amazed as they were.

One child opened a window, letting in sunlight that glistened and sparkled on the webs, creating beautiful colors of silver and gold and making the tree twinkle as if it had candles in it. Everyone was delighted and grateful for this lovely gift that the spiders had left for them. They realized that while they were poor, they were rich in other ways.

And this is why many Ukrainians now put spiderweb ornaments in their Christmas trees: to remind them to be grateful for what they have, and that precious gifts don't have to be expensive or lavish. And all because of the generosity of a few kind spiders!

An old superstition in Ukraine, Germany, and Poland says that it's good luck to find a spider web or even an actual spider in your Christmas tree. And it's also possible that the mainstream tradition of adorning Christmas trees with tinsel is a remnant of this old belief in the beauty of spiderwebs, so just keep that in mind the next time you're decorating your tree!

Svyatki

Russia

Svyatki runs later than many of the other celebrations outlined here, stretching from Orthodox Christmas Eve (January 7) until Orthodox Epiphany (January 19). As is the case in many of these holidays, such as Twelfth Night, Svyatki is set aside for celebrations, some of which are church-approved and some of which are most definitely not. Traditionally, this was a time when the sun had already "returned" and the days were beginning to grow noticeably longer. The word itself comes from svyatoy, or "holy," which is a little ironic, considering the pre-Christian elements of the merrymaking, but also the sheer amount of naughty behavior that ensued.

In Russia, this time was celebrated with lavish festivities and, if possible, feasts to ring in the New Year and to inspire hope for a good year to come. But it was also said to be a time when all of the devils were let loose to cause mischief and worse. In commemoration of this, young people would dress up in old rags, pointy hats, and scary masks, a practice we've seen over and over in this book. They would make loud noises, sing lewd songs, shout, and cause general mayhem, trying to provoke trouble and scare people. They would also go from door to door, asking for gifts and treats. It was unwise to refuse their demands, because giving these kids gifts ensured a lucky year ahead. Pranksters might also knock things over, smear soot or even manure on people, and wake them up in the middle of the night—all in good fun, of course!

This was also a time when dead ancestors would return to visit the living. At the major celebration feasts, such as Christmas Eve and Epiphany, people would not clear the tables after

the meal, in case the dead wanted to drop by for a bite to eat. People also staged mock funerals in welcome. They would dress a boy in white, powder his face with flour, and insert false teeth into his mouth made of a vegetable, such as a turnip. Someone dressed as a priest would burn manure in an incense holder (that must have smelled wonderful), and carry out a mock rite for the dead to symbolize the passing of the old year. As you can imagine, not many houses would want to host an event like this, so the young people would sometimes try to find an abandoned building to carry out this less-than-appealing ritual.

Teenage boys and girls would sometimes use these days as a chance to play lewd games with each other that they couldn't get away with during the rest of the year: things involving groping, head butting, catcalling, and other interactions that adults frowned upon but seemed to have been willing to over-look during this time. Boys would sometimes get into vodka-induced brawls, and girls would take up fortune-telling. The church forbade this, but again, it tended to look the other way for a few weeks. Girls would go to crossroads or rivers, where spirits were thought to dwell. One version involved bravely sticking one's hand into a bathhouse in the dark. If something with a hairy hand or paw touched their hand, their future hus-band would be rich, but if the skin was smooth, he would be poor. Undoubtedly, boys hid in these places and tried to scare the girls silly! These girls might also try to catch a glimpse of a future husband though a hole in the ice, but they were always to carry a cross or even a rooster to scare away evil spirits that were drawn to them.

Svyatki has many of the same characteristics of other dark hol-iday festivities, but adds in its own unique cultural flair, too. Seriously, burning manure?!

Korochun

Slavic Countries

Korochun is also known as Koliada, and refers to various Slavic celebrations that occur at about the same time as Svyatki. Versions of these festivities can be found in Ukraine, Belarus, Bulgaria, Macedonia, Poland, Lithuania, Romania, the Czech Republic, Slovakia, Slovenia, and elsewhere.

Korochun might originally have been a pagan celebration, a time when it was believed the so-called "Black God" walked the earth. This god, known as Chernobog, was a source of great evil, and when he wandered over the lands, everyone cowed in fear. According to a twelfth-century monk, the pagan Slavs believed that Chernobog was opposed by a light god, Belobog, from whom all goodness came. Later writers from the sixteenth and seventeenth centuries repeated these claims, and for a while it was thought that these two were indeed major deities that the pagan Slavs worshipped and feared.

The problem is, as cool as this sounds, there is no good evidence that these two were ever seen as gods, or that Belobog existed at all, for that matter. It's entirely possible that Chernobog was instead a vague notion of bad luck, and that Belobog was invented later by Christian writers to create a kind of God/devil opposition. Chernobog as a concept might have been "satanized" by the church to make the idea seem even more fearful.

So while it would be cool to think that the pagan Slavs viewed late December as the time when their most feared deity came down to the mortal realm to bring havoc and ruin, there isn't any good evidence for it. But that doesn't mean that Koruchun wasn't celebrated in other ways. Pagan Slavs seem to have thought of the time as one for remembering their ancestors, lighting fires for them, and perhaps trying to communicate with them. And certainly, Koliada is still a big deal for the Slavic peoples, just as all of the other festivals outlined here are for their various celebrants.

The word might refer to the idea of a reborn sun god named Kolyada, but it also is the name of a sun goddess who is responsible for sunrise, just to confuse things a little. There's no doubt that Koliada celebrations date back to before the coming of Christianity.

So what happens during Koliada? Many of the same things that we find across Europe: costumes, singing and dancing, going door-to-door for treats, colorful parades, feasting, and enjoyment of all kinds. In the Ukrainian version, there is also often a procession for a sacrificial goat—not a real goat, of course (though it probably was in earlier times), but a person dressed up as a goat, who dances for an abundant spring and a good harvest. He is symbolically killed by other revelers dressed as wolves and/or hunters, but then springs to life again when a group of singers call him back. He then is led around as a hopeful symbol that the fields will be fertile and a good year will follow.

There are games, bonfires, lewd jokes, many different kinds of fortune-telling, and, in some countries, food is left out for the dead. It's all wonderfully pagan and shows how different beliefs and cultures can synthesize into new traditions. The church knew it could never wipe out these celebrations completely, so it had to accommodate them and co-opt them. Koliada, like so many of the revels we've seen, is a mix of old and new.

Santa Kuroshu and Other Traditions

Japan

While the majority of Japan's population follows either Shinto or Buddhism, or both, Christmas has become an increasingly popular holiday in the country, for many of the same reasons that it is popular in a lot of nonmajority Christian countries: the colors, lights, spectacle, feasts, and general celebrations. As we've seen, winter is a time for gatherings and feasts, as well as a harsh reminder of the dangers and even death that could await the unwary. So many of the winter monsters we've met in this book hearken back to those times, when getting through the cold months was an uncertain prospect at best.

So while Japan has its own ways of marking winter, especially in the colder, snowier north, many people have happily taken to a lot of the European and American imagery that now goes with the Christmas season. And that includes Santa Claus. The Japanese version of the jolly old elf is known as Santa Kuroshu, who is basically like the familiar versions of Santa, but with one weird and creepy exception. He has eyes in the back of his head. Like, literally, he has eyes in the back of his head. This is to let children know that he is always watching and can tell if they're being naughty or nice.

Interestingly, children usually believe that only Santa Kuroshu can give gifts, so they don't give gifts to their parents. Additionally, if a child doesn't believe in Santa Kuroshu, he or she will not receive any gifts that year.

In some places, Santa Kuroshu is identified with Hotei, one of the chubby "laughing Buddhas" of traditional Japanese Buddhism, who was known to bring gifts of food and drink for New Year celebrations. It was obviously not a big step to combine him with Santa.

The big day tends to be Christmas Eve, rather than Christmas Day. People enjoy a sponge cake covered with strawberries and, if possible, a traditional meal of...Kentucky Fried Chicken. Yes, somehow, KFC has become the go-to destination for many people's holiday feasts, whether dining in or taking out. Turkey is not a common or easy-to-find bird in Japan, so chicken is the next logical substitute. In fact, the restaurant chain is so popular now that people have to make Christmas Eve reservations long in advance to get seats if they want to dine in. Score one for fast food.

One other interesting fact: if you're sending Christmas cards to anyone in Japan, avoid having the color red on them, since it has associations with death. While red is generally a very lucky color in Japanese culture, funeral notices are also often sent in red, so it's probably the last thing you want to be wishing for your friends during the holiday season!

Yuki-onna

Japan

Yuki-onna ("snow woman") isn't specifically Christmas-related, but she is a type of winter spirit that is sorrowful and frequently terrifying, and might well be glimpsed at that time of year. While the Japanese love Christmas celebrations, they are also mindful of their own rich and often frightening folklore. She often appears in the second half of January, a time when traditionally there were New Year celebrations, so, as with European legends, we see a connection between a time of revelry and a sometimes-horrid ghoul that would arrive to spoil the fun.

She usually appears as a beautiful young woman with long black hair, dressed all in white, seemingly one with the snow itself. There are many legends about her, and these can range from sweet to sorrowful to horrifying, depending on the regions where she pops up. It's not quite clear what Yuki-onna is. Some tales say that she was a young woman who perished in a snowstorm, or was led into a forest in winter and murdered, while others say that she originally dwelled among the gods or on the moon. She came down to Earth to experience this world, but was trapped here and now cannot leave. Any of these reasons could be enough to make her a spirit of murderous vengeance.

Legends about Yuki-onna date back to at least the fifteenth century, when an acclaimed poet named Sōgi claimed to have seen her. He said that she was at least ten feet tall, with completely white skin, but when he tried to speak with her, she vanished.

Her stories are both sad and sometimes violent, a warning to all who venture out into the cold nights of a Japanese winter. And yet, some of her appearances are fairly benign. She might be seen asking for water. If given cold water, she grows in size, but if given hot water, she evaporates. Other tales tell how she knocked at the door of an older man's home, asking to be let in to warm up. The home's owner did this, and she stayed for a time, and then went to leave. When he tried to stop her and took hold of her hand, it was ice cold. She then transformed into a burst of snow and drifted up the chimney.

Other stories are less wistful. Sometimes she appears to travelers with a child, asking them to hug it. If they do, the child and the hugger will become covered with ice and snow and the unfortunate mortal will freeze to death. If the person refuses to hug the child, Yuki-onna will shove them over the edge of the nearest hill, to plunge to their deaths.

Sometimes Yuki-onna haunts forests, actively seeking out victims. When someone comes by, she will attack and freeze them, and then suck the *seiki*, or essence, out of their mouths, leaving them a frozen husk. Children have especially desirable *seiki*, apparently. Some legends of the malicious Yuki-onna say that she enjoys ripping the livers out of their victims, but almost all of them include her freezing her captives to death in one way or another. Other tales of Yuki-onna say that she will call out to a traveler, and if that person answers, she will attack. On the other hand, different legends warn that she will call out to a traveler, and if that person ignores her, she will attack! So basically, you can't win and the real lesson here is stay home when it's snowing at night.

La Quema del Diablo

Guatemala

On December 7 at precisely 6:00 p.m., the people of Guatemala take part in an annual ritual across the country, most notably at the Barrio de La Concepción in La Antigua. Known as La Quema del Diablo, or "The Burning of the Devil," it's a celebration in preparation for the Feast of the Immaculate Conception the following day. At that time, a full-sized paper model of the devil (but how do they know how big the devil is, anyway?) is brought out and presented to the huge crowds, and then ritually burned.

This particular gathering of people has only been around since the 1990s, though the tradition of burning (presumably) smaller images of the devil dates back to at least the eighteenth century. The ritual was held at that time to purge the home of evil spirits and ensure that, with the onset of the Christmas season, the house would get off to a good start in the New Year, and that evil would be driven away in anticipation of Jesus's birth.

Originally, the act took place in monasteries, the monks burning the devil in effigy and lighting fireworks for the Day of Mary, Queen of the Rosary, on October 7. The tradition was later moved to December to make it fit in with Christmas celebrations and the Immaculate Conception.

While the big celebration goes on in the city, people elsewhere will buy or build their own devils made of papier-mâché or wood. On the appointed day, they will collect burnable trash and assemble makeshift pyres in the streets, often with firefighters standing by, just in case the devil decides he doesn't

like this treatment and tries to take revenge. Then, dousing their figures with gasoline or other combustibles, they set the devil alight and burn away all the problems of the old year (both real and in the mind), reducing them to nothing but ash. Sometimes, they even place firecrackers inside or beside their devils for an extra kick. And with that, the holiday season can begin in earnest.

But the tradition is not without controversy. The dangers of fires getting out of hand in neighborhoods with limited fire-fighting forces are an obvious problem, and all of the smoke created from the fires can be choking and an environmental safety issue, making the air difficult to breathe and polluting it with potentially toxic chemicals from burning garbage (people have a tendency to burn anything they want to get rid of, regardless of whether this is safe or not). There have been moves to abolish the celebration altogether, or replace it with something else. One suggestion has been for celebrants to replace the burning devils with devil piñatas. These satanic effigies can be whacked and bashed with abandon (and may be filled with treats), thus giving an alternative violent way to start the season's festivities. But will the people take to this newer, safer tradition? Time will tell.

The Modern Mystery of Danny the Ghost

South Africa...or Not

South African Christmas traditions aren't all that different from those in Europe and elsewhere, owing to the presence of Dutch colonists and later internationalization. And of course, some European foods and celebrations have been mixed with traditional African ones, giving the holiday its own unique identity. But according to a few sources, the country does have one weird and twisted urban legend that might have children telling and retelling it to scare the life out of each other as the most anticipated day of the year approaches.

According to the story, a young boy named Danny loved cookies, and his grandmother had baked a batch for the family, a few of which were to be left out for Santa. She warned him that he was not to eat any of them until the appointed time, since they were meant for a special purpose. But boys being boys, Danny decided to sneak at least a few of them (or perhaps all?) when he thought he wouldn't be caught. And of course, grandma found out and she gave him a beating so terrible that it killed him. As such, Danny's ghost cannot find rest and now haunts houses to warn other children not to do what he did. If they do, he might just kill them, too!

It's a great story that fits in well with the other ghoulish December delights we've explored in this book. The problem is, it doesn't seem to be an authentic story at all, at least not one that circulates among the young people of South Africa. Some researchers have tried to track down the original version of this urban legend, but apparently, no one in South Africa has heard of it! So, it seems that this story was made up online in 2015 (there are a few possible origins that sleuths have identified). The tale might have even been planted deliberately as a falsehood to see if others copied it and shared it. It is not, alas, a tale that kids share to scare.

That might take some of the fun out of it, but in reality, that's how new traditions and legends are born. Somebody, somewhere, makes something up, and before long, people are repeating it, embellishing it, and adapting it to their own circumstances. There's no reason that this particular story has to be set in South Africa, for example. It's universal and has a lot of the same themes as any haunting holiday horror story.

The story of Danny's ghost is a new folktale that might yet find its way into regular rotation as a good ghost story to tell every year, to scare children into being good. Or it might vanish and be forgotten, but there is no doubt that other terrifying tales will take hold over time.

About the Author

Tim Rayborn has a lifelong interest in (obsession with, really) the unusual, the strange, the bizarre, and the rather creepy. He has written several books on these topics, including *The Big Book of Paranormal*, *A History of the End of the World*, and *Beethoven's Skull*, among many others. He's actually written a huge number of books (nearly fifty at present!) and magazine articles (more than thirty!) on subjects such as music, the arts, general knowledge, fantasy fiction, the whole weird and unknown thing, and history of all kinds.

He is planning to write more books, whether anyone wants him to or not. He lived in England for several years and studied at the University of Leeds for his PhD, which means he likes to pretend that he knows what he's talking about.

He's also an almost-famous musician who plays many unusual instruments from all over the world that most people have never heard of and usually can't pronounce. He has appeared on more than forty recordings, and his musical wanderings and tours have taken him across the U.S., all over Europe, to Canada and Australia, and to such romantic locations as Umbrian medieval towns, Marrakech, Vienna, Renaissance chateaux, medieval churches, and high school gymnasiums.

He currently lives in rainy Washington State with many books, recordings, and instruments.

www.timrayborn.com

About Cider Mill Press Book Publishers

Good ideas ripen with time. From seed to harvest, Cider Mill Press brings fine reading, information, and entertainment together between the covers of its creatively crafted books. Our Cider Mill bears fruit twice a year, publishing a new crop of titles each spring and fall.

CIDER MILL
PRESS

BOOK
PUBLISHERS

"Where Good Books Are Ready for Press"

501 Nelson Place
Nashville, Tennessee 37214

cidermillpress.com

Printed in the USA
CPSIA information can be obtained
at www.ICGtesting.com
LVHW060027311223
767076LV00013B/186